Sophie's Stormy Summer

Other books in the growing Faithgirlz!™ library

Best Friends Bible

The Sophie Series

Sophie's World (Book One)
Sophie's Secret (Book Two)
Sophie and the Scoundrels (Book Three)
Sophie's Irish Showdown (Book Four)
Sophie's First Dance (Book Five)
Sophie Breaks the Code (Book Seven)
Sophie Tracks a Thief (Book Eight)

Nonfiction

No Boys Allowed: Devotions for Girls
Girlz Rock: Devotions for You

Check out www.faithgirlz.com

faiThGirLz!

Sophie's Stormy Summer
Nancy Rue

Zonderkidz

Zonder**kidz**®

The children's group of Zondervan

www.zonderkidz.com

Sophie's Stormy Summer
Copyright © 2005 by Nancy Rue

Requests for information should be addressed to:
Zonderkidz, 5300 Patterson Ave. SE
Grand Rapids, Michigan 49530

Library of Congress Cataloging-in-Publication Data

Rue, Nancy N.
Sophie's stormy summer / Nancy Rue.
     p. cm.–(Faithgirlz)
     Summary: The Corn Flakes are devastated to learn that Kitty has cancer, but when summer vacations separate them and put their new film on hold, Sophie determines to do anything God calls her to do to make Kitty feel better--even give up her beautiful hair.
     ISBN 10: 0-310-70761-7 (softcover)
     ISBN 13: 978-0-310-70761-5 (softcover)
     [1. Cancer—Fiction. 2. Diseases—Fiction. 3. Sick—Fiction. 4. Friendship—Fiction.
5. Christian life—Fiction. 6. Imagination—Fiction.] I. Title. II. Series.
     PZ7.R88515Sn 2005
     [Fic]–dc22

                 2004030899

Published in association with the literary agency of Alive Communications, Inc., 7680 Goddard Street, Suite 200, Colorado Springs, CO 80920.

Photography: Synergy Photographic/Brad Lampe
Illustrations: Grace Chen Design & Illustration
Art direction/design: Michelle Lenger
Interior design: Susan Ambs
Interior composition: Susan Ambs

Printed in the United States of America

---

05 06 07 08 09/❖DCI/5 4 3 2 1

So we fix our eyes not on what is seen, but on what is unseen. For what is seen is temporary, but what is unseen is eternal.

—*2 Corinthians 4:18*

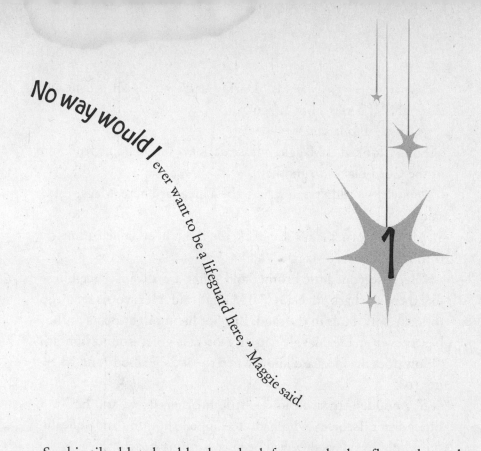

No way would I ever want to be a lifeguard here," Maggie said.

1

Sophie tilted her head back to look from under her floppy hat at her getting-tanner-by-the-minute friends.

Sophie's best-best friend, Fiona, didn't look up from the miniature hut they were building in the sand with dried seaweed sticks. She kept poking them in the sand with one hand while she brushed the usual strand of hair out of one eye with the other. "Why not, Mags?" she said.

Kitty wrinkled her made-like-china nose, now spattered with freckles. "I wouldn't want to *be* a lifeguard, but I might want to be *saved* by one." Her dark ponytail bounced as she giggled— which she did at the end of almost every sentence.

"Of course you would," Darbie said, her Irish accent lilting through. "If it was a boy lifeguard."

"Gross," Fiona said.

Sophie looked at Maggie, whose dark eyes were going from one of the Corn Flakes to another.

"So why wouldn't you want to be a lifeguard here, Mags?" she said.

All the Corn Flakes sat back on their heels and squinted through the sun at Maggie.

"Because your little brother and sister are always screaming like there's a shark attack 24/7," Maggie said. Her words seemed to make soft thuds in the sand. But Sophie thought being at the beach even made Maggie's matter-of-fact voice sound lighter. "How does the lifeguard know when to save somebody and when not to?"

She nodded toward Fiona's little brother, Rory, and her even littler sister, Isabella, who hadn't stopped shouting and squealing the whole five days they had been at Virginia Beach.

"Izzy and Rory *have* to make all those sounds at the seashore because they're little," Sophie said. She had also felt like holding her arms out to the ocean and squealing several times since she and the Corn Flakes had been there, and she was TWELVE. It was as if the waves themselves, tumbling over one another like puppies, were setting her free. Well, that and the fact that she was here with the four people in the whole world she could be herself with.

Sure, we're flakes, Sophie thought happily. *And we do corny stuff—but we are who we are.*

"At least they're making happy noises for a change," Darbie said, nodding toward Izzy and Rory. "Usually they're shrieking like terrorists." She clapped a sunblock-shiny hand over her mouth and looked quickly at Fiona's mother. "No offense, Dr. Bunting," she said through her fingers. "They're perfectly charming."

Dr. Bunting pulled off her sunglasses and turned to Darbie. "You were right the first time. They are little terrorists."

"What I can't get," Fiona said, "is why they always have to be throwing something—buckets, sand, food—on each OTHER." She sighed out loud. "It's heinous."

Dr. Bunting blinked her gray-like-Fiona's eyes and put her sunglasses back on. "If tossing a few Cheetos is the worst those two do before we leave here, it's because Miss Genevieve is the nanny from heaven."

"I thought we were supposed to call her the *au pair*," Maggie said.

"Just call me Genevieve." The blonde, creamy-skinned woman who was on her knees making castle towers pointed a graceful finger at Rory. "Get more of that sand you just gave me," she said to him. "With it just wet enough, we can build anything."

Rory trotted obediently toward the water with his bucket and shovel, and Dr. Bunting looked out from under the brim of her white visor. "See what I mean?" she said.

Sophie tried to imagine Fiona's last nanny playing at the beach with Rory and Izzy dumping seashells over each other's heads. Miss Odetta Clide had handed out demerits if they spilled their milk. True, she had turned out to be less like a steel rod than they'd thought at first, but she NEVER would have gotten on her hands and knees in the sand.

The Corn Flakes—including their newest member, Willoughby—had all been worried about who would take Miss Odetta Clide's place when she married Fiona's grandfather Boppa, and they went off to Europe on their honeymoon for the summer. With Fiona's parents taking all of the girls—except Willoughby, who was on vacation with her family—to Virginia Beach for ten whole days, the choice of a nanny would determine the amount of fun they could have.

Sophie watched Genevieve drip wet sand through her hand to create a castle tower, the way soft ice cream piled on top of a cone. The au pair's thick braid hung over her shoulder like a silk rope, and her blue eyes seemed to hug Isabella as the curly-headed four-year-old tried to dribble sand through her tiny fingers. *I want to be like Genevieve when I grow up,* Sophie thought. *IF I grow up.*

Not that she WANTED to—at least not right now. Here—building a little beach hut out of dried sticks of seaweed with her best friends, she didn't have to think about anything scary, like starting middle school in two months . . .

"Okay," Sophie said out loud. "Everybody tell their favorite part about being at the beach so far."

Fiona pushed a stubborn strand of golden-brown hair behind one ear as she poked the sticks into the adobe-colored sand like she was doing math. "I liked it when we dug those giant bowls in the sand and climbed in there, all of us together."

"We KILLED ourselves laughing over things that are funny only to us," Darbie said.

"Was that your favorite too?" Sophie said to her.

Darbie kept weaving seaweed into the roof of their masterpiece for a minute. Her reddish hair and her snapping eyes were as dark as her flesh was white. She was the one most likely to burn like a marshmallow. Sophie liked to think of Darbie running on the beaches of Northern Ireland where she had lived until last year, shouting things like "blackguards"—which Darbie pronounced as "blaggards" and meant people who did evil things.

"My favorite," Darbie said finally, "was when we used those long sticks to write our names on the beach—and the shells were our periods and commas." She grinned her crooked-toothed smile. "At least, the shells we're not taking home by the bucketful to Poquoson."

"I liked pelican-watching," Maggie said. She was just returning to the job site with a bucket full of dried seaweed, her face Maggie-solemn, as if she were doing serious business. "I liked watching them fish."

"I DIDN'T like that part," Kitty said. "We only did that when Genevieve made us wait thirty minutes after we ate before we could go back in the water."

Maggie cocked her head at Kitty, so that her blunt-cut shiny hair splashed against her face just below her ears. "You have to do that," she said. "Or you'll get a cramp and drown."

Sophie squinted her brown eyes through her glasses at Kitty. "So what WAS your favorite?"

"It's too hard to pick," Kitty said. Her curly ponytail bounced on the breeze, and at that moment, Sophie thought, *I want her, I want ALL of us, to stay just like we are. And I want everything we ever do together to be as perfect as it is right now.*

"While you're thinking about it, Kitty," Fiona said, "we need more seashells for furniture."

"Why do *I* have to get them?" Kitty went straight into whining mode. To a certain degree, as Fiona always said, that was just Kitty's usual voice, just like Maggie's dropped out in matter-of-fact blocks, and Sophie's was as high-pitched and squeaky as a caught mouse. But right now Kitty suddenly had an I'm-about-to-cry edge to her voice.

"You don't have to get them," Fiona said, her own voice cheery. "You can just stand there and watch while we do all the work."

"Don't yell at me, Fiona," Kitty said.

"Who's yelling?" Fiona looked blankly at Sophie. "Was I yelling?"

"All right, I'll get more seashells, Kitty," Darbie said. "And you keep making the entrance."

"What entrance?"

"Right here," Maggie said.

She pointed to the sticks, like soft bamboo, that Sophie had laid crosswise between two rows of those stuck upright into the sand. *No offense, Kitty,* Sophie thought, *but we've been making it since lunch. Hello?*

Genevieve hadn't let them go back into the water after they'd eaten their sandwiches because she'd spotted jags of lightning so far away that Fiona said the rest of them would need the Hubble Telescope to see them. But when Genevieve had shown them how to make exotic-looking buildings, their claims that they were going to "go mental" if they couldn't go swimming had faded.

"It isn't rocket science," Fiona said to Kitty. "Just put them in there."

"I'm not stupid, Fiona!" Kitty said. "You always make me feel stupid!"

Sophie could hear the Kitty-tears getting closer, and she crawled over to Kitty and put her arm around her. Kitty usually put her head on Sophie's shoulder when she did that, but Sophie could feel her cringing.

"What's wrong?" Sophie said.

"Is it a sand issue?" Darbie said. "I hate when it gets in my bathing suit—especially right where it's sunburned at the edges."

"No!" Kitty said. "It's everybody being mean to me!"

Dr. Bunting toyed with a gold hoop earring as she studied Kitty. "Define 'mean,'" she said.

"I can't!" Kitty said—and she pulled her sandy hands over her eyes and burst into tears.

Dr. Bunting looked at Genevieve. "Oh, those preadolescent hormones," she said.

Genevieve lifted her chin—chiseled out of pure marble, Sophie was sure—as if she were listening to something.

"Thunder," she said. "Time to move indoors."

"No!" Rory said.

"Yes," Genevieve said.

"Okay," Rory said.

"If you can do that, you can stop a storm, Genevieve," Dr. Bunting said.

"What storm?" Fiona said.

Sophie looked up. The sky was like a moving watercolor picture, all in grays, and the wind was delivering karate chops to the water.

"I felt a raindrop," Maggie said.

"Wasn't that just spray from the ocean?" Darbie said. "Isn't that what it was, Fiona?"

"No," Maggie said. "It's rain."

"Thanks, Mags," Fiona said, grinning. "You're tons of help."

"Everyone pack up what you carried down, and let's head to the house," Genevieve said.

"Can somebody else do mine?" Kitty said. "I'm too tired—I can't."

"I will," Sophie said—before Fiona could set her sobbing again.

"You're barely big enough to carry your own stuff, Little Bit," Fiona's mom said to Sophie. "What's the deal, Kitty?"

Kitty dropped onto a cooler and put her face in her hands again. By then, the wind was scattering the beach hut and kicking sand over Kitty's beach tote.

"I'll get that," Darbie said.

Maggie didn't say anything. She just knelt down with her back to Kitty, and Kitty climbed on. Plodding through the sand, Maggie headed up the beach.

"You go ahead with her," Genevieve said to the rest of them.

Genevieve rolled Izzy into a towel like a burrito, handed her to Dr. Bunting, and then put Rory up on her shoulders. Darbie,

Sophie, and Fiona hoisted their own burdens on themselves like pack mules and started for the big wooden house. Its wide windows looked sightlessly down at them as the rain began to slash against the glass.

Sophie had to take off her hat so it wouldn't get blown away, and her hair whipped across her face. A pair of windshield wipers for her glasses would have been nice. But there was something about the sudden storm that prickled her skin with excitement.

"Let's pretend we've been shipwrecked!" she shouted to the girls.

"And that house is our only refuge!" Darbie shouted back.

"The only problem," Fiona cried over the wind-howl, "is that the place is full of pirates!"

Sophie raised a fist above her head. "We have no other choice! We must survive!"

"Help, Kitty!" Maggie cried out. "Help her!"

Kitty's finally getting into it, Sophie thought. Kitty was sprawled out in the sand, and Maggie threw herself down beside her.

"Now is NOT a good time to start acting it out!" Darbie called to Maggie.

"I'm not acting! There's something wrong with her!"

Sophie only stared for a second before she dumped her tote and the basket of chip bags and churned her feet in the sand to get to Kitty. She fell on her knees next to her and let her breath go with the wind.

Kitty lay on her back; face gray like ashes. Sophie put her hand on her arm, and Kitty winced and her face twisted into a knot, but she didn't pull away.

It was as if she couldn't.

"Please don't touch me," Kitty said. "It hurts. It hurts."

Fiona was suddenly holding her rolled-up little sister, and Dr. Bunting was on the

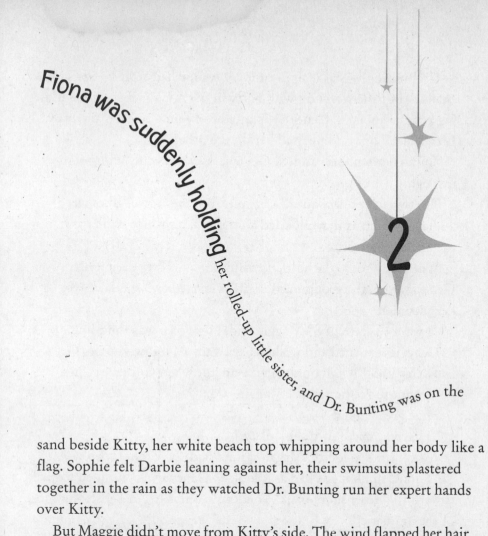

sand beside Kitty, her white beach top whipping around her body like a flag. Sophie felt Darbie leaning against her, their swimsuits plastered together in the rain as they watched Dr. Bunting run her expert hands over Kitty.

But Maggie didn't move from Kitty's side. The wind flapped her hair against the side of her face, and yet she stayed still as a stone.

"Let's get you into the house, Kitty-Cat," Dr. Bunting finally shouted to Kitty.

"It hurts to move!"

"That's why I'm going to carry you. Up we go."

Dr. Bunting was as lean as runners Sophie had seen on the sports channel, but she stood up with Kitty in her arms as if she were lifting a bag of sponges. Genevieve shifted Rory onto one hip and took Izzy from Fiona and planted her on the other.

"Heads down, everyone!" Genevieve called out. "Plow right through!"

The two little ones squealed happily. But the Corn Flakes were a solemn group as they plodded after them, faces cowering from the bite of the storm.

When they got to the house, Dr. Bunting and Kitty disappeared. Genevieve led the group inside. "Showers, ladies," she said over her shoulder.

"I want to see Kitty," Maggie said. Her voice was thudding.

Genevieve turned and walked backward. "I know you do. Get showered and I'll find out from the doctor when you can see her."

"I want to see her now," Maggie said.

"Just give it a few—"

"I have to make sure she's okay."

"My mom's a doctor, Mags!" Fiona said. "Of course she's okay."

"I don't think it's as bad as it looks." Genevieve continued to back toward the downstairs hall. "You know our Kitty has a strong sense of the dramatic."

"What does that mean?" Maggie said as the Corn Flakes climbed the stairs to their suite.

"It means Kitty's a drama queen," Fiona said. "Which is our own fault. We made her that way."

"She'll be up making our film with us before supper," Sophie said to Maggie. "You know she will."

"No, I don't," Maggie said. "And neither do you. You didn't see her when she fell down. She went limp—like this."

Maggie demonstrated on the stair landing. *We made HER a drama queen too*, Sophie thought.

"I did that when I had a bad dose of flu," Darbie said.

"Yeah, I bet she's got the flu," Fiona said. "She was sick the week before we came. Her mom almost didn't let her go with us, but since my mom's a doctor she said it was okay."

Maggie looked at each one of them as they spoke, but nothing on her face was moving.

Darbie put her hand up to her mouth. Sophie could hear a laugh bubbling up her throat.

"It's not funny," Maggie said.

"Not that! Look at us!" Darbie said. "We're all in flitters—we look as if we washed up onshore and some old beach bum dragged us in!"

Sophie looked at the four of them and started her own fit of giggles. Their hair was all soaked and matted to their heads, and their suits and T-shirts drooped on them like hung-up laundry.

"Do I look as funny as you guys do?" Fiona said. She ran to the mirrors on the closet doors and shrieked at herself. "I'm hideous!"

"I'm a sea witch!" Sophie squeaked at her own reflection.

Even Maggie's lips twitched as she stared at her wilted self. "I'm taking a shower," she said. "I'm gross."

Clean and combed and equipped with juice boxes and tortilla chips and the homemade salsa Maggie's mom had sent along, the girls were in the big second-floor sunroom watching the ocean whip into a frenzy when Genevieve came in. She looked as if she'd never even been in the storm. She was in jean shorts and a stretchy T-shirt with lime green flip-flops to match.

"Can I go see Kitty now?" Maggie said.

Genevieve smiled at her. "You have a mind like a steel trap. Dr. Bunting's still with her. What's good to eat?"

"What's wrong with her?" Maggie said.

"She's not sure yet," Genevieve said, smiling again and scooping a handful of chips.

"But you know something."

Sophie thought Maggie was right. Genevieve was acting the way adults did when they were trying to change the subject—being all thrilled over something like chips and making their voices cheery.

"Someone's perceptive," Genevieve said. She sighed. "Kitty's running a fever. Mr. Bunting is calling her parents to see if they want to come get her, take her to her own doctor."

"My mom's a great doctor!" Fiona said.

"The best. But she doesn't have all the equipment here to run tests."

"Why do they have to run tests for the flu?" Fiona said.

"It must be a REALLY bad dose," Darbie said.

Maggie shook her head. "It's not the flu."

Genevieve's eyes sparkled at Maggie as she nibbled on the tip of a chip. "You're a doctor now too."

"Doctors don't get all concerned about the flu," Maggie said. "She's bad off sick."

"She's not that sick, Mags," Fiona said.

"You don't know."

"Guys—," Sophie said.

"You know a lot of stuff," Maggie said. "But you can't know this—"

"Guys—"

"We all get fevers. Darbie—when was your last fever?"

"Guys!"

They all stopped and looked at Sophie. She tried to wind her voice down out of squeak zone.

"Maybe we should just pray," she said. "That's what Dr. Peter would say."

"But first—fill me in," Genevieve said. "Dr. Peter's your Bible study teacher, right?"

Everyone started to talk at once—except Maggie—and Genevieve finally held her hand up to shush them all, and pointed to Sophie.

"You tell, Cuteness," she said.

So Sophie cleared up everything about Dr. Peter, the Christian therapist her parents started sending her to see almost a year ago when she had been spending most of her time daydreaming. Now she was seeing him only once a month, but Darbie talked to him almost every week, because she had a lot of things to deal with—like her father's dying in Northern Ireland when she was just a baby, and her having to grow up with violence on the streets, and then her mother's being killed in a car accident so that she had to come to the United States to live with her aunt and uncle in Poquoson. Dr. Peter was the best, the best, the best at helping kids work out their stuff. He'd even gotten Maggie to start eating again, back at the end of the sixth grade, when nobody else could.

And now, Sophie explained to Genevieve, Dr. Peter had their new Bible study group at church, which they just called their Girls Group, where they were learning how to be close to God by getting to know Jesus—big breath—by studying the Bible and learning that it showed them how to live. All the Corn Flakes went to the class, except for Kitty.

"Her parents don't believe in church," Sophie said.

Darbie lowered her voice to a whisper. "We're not even sure they believe in God."

Genevieve nodded. Not a single smirk or "isn't that cute" had appeared on her face while Sophie was talking.

"Then that's all the more reason to pray for her," she said. "Do you join hands or what?"

They always did, and they did it now, and with Sophie starting they all asked God, one by one, to be with Kitty and not let her be afraid. Maggie just flat out TOLD God that he had to make Kitty better fast.

When they all opened their eyes, Genevieve still had hers closed. Sophie waited until she lifted her eyelids.

"What were you praying there at the end?" Sophie said.

"I don't think you can ask someone that, Sophie!" Darbie said, pronouncing Sophie's name the way she always did, like it rhymed with "goofy."

Fiona grinned. "She's just inquisitive."

"What's 'inquisitive'?" Maggie said.

"I ask a lot of questions." Sophie pushed her glasses up her nose. "Is that okay, Genevieve?"

"It is absolutely okay. There at the end, I was just imagining Jesus."

Darbie practically knocked over the salsa dish. "That's what Dr. Peter taught us to do!"

Genevieve daintily chewed a chip. "I learned it from my grandmother, my mother's mother. It's what got her through some pretty horrible times in her life."

"What happened to her?" Sophie said.

Fiona nodded. "Definitely inquisitive."

Genevieve dusted the salt from her hands over the table and wiped it with a napkin. She made it look like a hand lotion commercial.

"My grandfather—her husband—was Jewish. They lived in the south of France when the Nazis occupied France during World War II."

"Oh," Fiona said. "The Holocaust." She turned to the Corn Flakes. "You know, when Adolf Hitler tried to have all the Jewish people killed."

Sophie found herself inching closer to Genevieve.

"Was your grandmother Jewish too?" Darbie said.

Genevieve shook her head. "No, but she thought what the Nazis were doing was—"

"Heinous," Fiona put in.

"And she refused to abandon my grandfather."

"Was your mother born yet?" Fiona said.

"No."

"Then we know it turned out okay, because if it didn't, there wouldn't be you." Fiona nodded as if that took care of that.

"Depends on what you mean by 'okay,'" Genevieve said. Her smile was turned down at the corners. "They weren't killed, but they went through horrible things that haunted them for the rest of their lives."

Sophie felt Darbie shudder beside her. "Could we not talk about this right now?"

"Actually," Genevieve said, crossing her legs in front of her, "I was thinking we should watch a movie. Who's up for *Ice Age*?"

Sophie didn't catch much of the movie. She was busy in the south of France—

Huddling with her mother in the dark, wet alley, the young woman trained her eyes to see at least the outline of her father. Her brave father, who had crept out to see if the Nazis were coming. "Father!" she hissed into the eerie mist. "Come back—they'll see you!" But there was no answer, no sign of her papa. "Mama," the French girl who didn't have a name yet said, "put your shawl over your head. Like this. Stay warm." She pulled the rough woolen shawl over her mother's head and tried not to see the frightened look in her eyes. She must stay brave.

"Sophie, why do you have that beach towel over your head?" Maggie said.

"Leave her alone, Mags," Fiona said. "It's our next film."

It was dark and they were starting *Ice Age* for the third time when Dr. Bunting let them see Kitty.

She was lying very still in the guestroom bed downstairs, just the way she had on the beach. When Fiona bounced onto the mattress beside her, Kitty winced as if Fiona had punched her out.

"She's achy," Dr. Bunting said.

"Like the flu," Darbie said.

Fiona looked at Maggie. "It IS the flu, right, Mom? I told Maggie it was."

"It hurts more than the flu," Kitty said. Sophie could barely hear her voice.

"Bad dose, then," Darbie said.

Maggie, meanwhile, was shifting her eyes between Kitty and Dr. Bunting.

"She has flu-like symptoms—," Dr. Bunting started to say.

But Fiona's father appeared in the doorway, looking tanned from the golf game he must have gotten rained out of, and tall and sort of ropey, as if he were all long, tight muscle. "Your dad's on his way, Kitty," he said.

"In this storm?" Maggie's eyebrows were twisted.

"I think your mom would do the same thing if you were sick," Dr. Bunting said. "Hey, why don't you guys keep Kitty company for a few minutes?"

She patted Kitty's hand and made her exit with Mr. Bunting right behind her. Sophie knew there was going to be a no-kids-allowed talk. It made her stomach uneasy.

"I don't want you to leave, Kitty!" Darbie said. "Sophie has a new idea for a flick. You should have seen her dreaming on it when we were watching *Ice Age*!"

"For the second AND third times," Fiona said.

"I'm sorry you missed it," Sophie said. "I know it's your favorite—but OUR film is going to be even better—"

"I don't want to go home," Kitty said.

At least she hadn't lost her whine. *That's probably why she's been thinking everybody's yelling at her*, Sophie thought. *She's been sick the whole time.*

"So beg your mom to let you stay," Fiona said. "My mom will take care of you."

"She's the one who said I have to go home."

"No way!" Fiona said. "Stay right here—I'll take care of this."

Fiona charged for the door, but her dad was already standing there. "It's a done deal, Fiona," he said. "So don't start giving me a five-point proposal."

"Let me just ask this one thing," Fiona said. "Why won't Mom take care of her? Will it interfere with her tan?"

Sophie sucked in a breath. She could picture herself talking to Daddy in that tone. She could also picture being grounded until she was in college.

But Fiona's father just said, "Step into my office, and we'll discuss it."

Fiona turned to the Corn Flakes and gave them a thumbs-up as she followed him into the hallway.

"Do you think she'll get him to let me stay?" Kitty said in her tiny voice. "If I go home, I'm going to miss everything!"

"No worries," Darbie said. "We won't have a bit of fun without you."

"I know I won't," Maggie said. Sophie could tell she meant it.

"It isn't fair!" Kitty said—and once again she started to cry. But it looked like it hurt to do that, and so she cried even harder.

"It's okay, Kitty," Sophie said. She got as close to the bed as she could without touching it. "We're only going to be here four more days. That'll give you time to get well so you can be in the film. We're all going to be French—what do you want your name to be?"

Kitty blinked. "Danielle. I always wanted to be called Danielle."

"I'll write that down in the book," Maggie said.

"I was Antoinette when we did our Williamsburg movie," Sophie said. "But I need to pick another name because this takes place during World War II, so Antoinette couldn't still be alive—at least, I don't think so—"

Kitty just watched her.

"We prayed for you," Sophie blurted out.

"It still works, even if you don't go to church," Darbie said. Then her face got blotchy-red and she gave Sophie a "Do something!" look.

Sophie didn't have to because Fiona came back in looking like something was pinching her face.

"My mom says we have to let Kitty sleep," she said.

"I'm not leaving," Maggie said.

"What if we're really quiet and we just sit here with her?" Darbie said.

Sophie didn't say anything. She knew Fiona. It wasn't just that she'd lost the battle with her parents. Something was very, very wrong.

Kitty's father arrived, still in his U.S. Air Force uniform, and when he walked into the house, Sophie felt like they should all jump to attention. The Corn Flakes followed him silently into the bedroom where he scooped the sleepy Kitty up in his beefy arms, ignored her whining to please let her stay, and told the Buntings he was sure she was going to be fine. He barked when he talked.

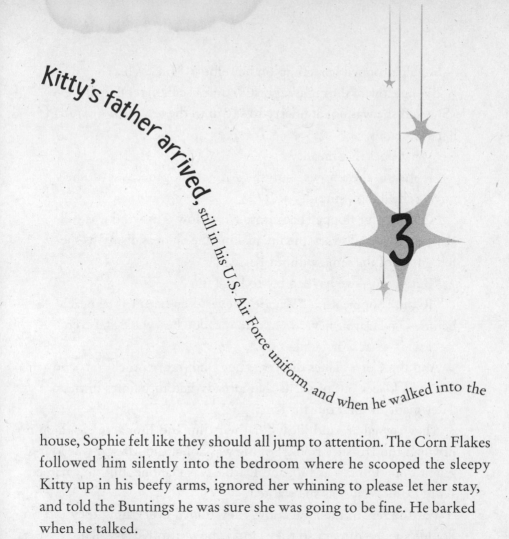

Only when they were gone and Maggie and Darbie were asleep did Fiona whisper to Sophie, "He told my dad he came to get her because he didn't want my parents to have to be taking care of her while they were on vacation. But my mom said she made him take her because she's sure Kitty has something worse than the flu."

Sophie propped herself up on her elbow. "Like what?"

By the glow of the nightlight, she could see Fiona rolling her eyes. "She said she was not at liberty to say until the test results confirm her suspicions."

"What does that mean?"

"It means she knows, but she's not telling because if she's wrong she'll look stupid."

"Oh." Sophie flopped back onto her pillow. The wind was still slapping the windows with rain, making the night as dismal as she felt. "It's not the same without Kitty."

"But, Soph—we have to try to have fun."

"Right," Sophie said. "Maggie's never even been to the beach before—and Darbie never went on a vacation her whole life, ever."

"Fun is what Corn Flakes do."

And the Corn Flakes did try. They built more beach huts and made necklaces out of shells that already had tiny holes in them. They made the best one for Kitty.

They tossed around ideas for their film and Fiona wrote them down in the Treasure Book. Sophie was Sofia, and Maggie was Marguerite, and Fiona was Fifi, and Darbie was Daphne. But they named Kitty Danielle, just as she wanted.

For the rest of their vacation, they filmed everything they did on Sophie's video camera so they could show it to Kitty when they got home. But when the camera was off, every time anybody brought up Kitty's name, they deflated a little, like air slowly being let out of a balloon.

Maggie asked Dr. Bunting at least four times a day whether she'd heard anything from Kitty's parents. Dr. Bunting always said no news was probably good news.

On their last day at the beach, the Corn Flakes were down at the water, saying good-bye to the ocean, when Maggie said, "Hey, Sophie. Your little brother's here."

Sophie whirled around to see six-year-old Zeke, dark brown hair sticking up in spikes, tearing down from the beach house with Izzy and Rory hot on his trail. Genevieve strode calmly behind them. Lacie, Sophie's fourteen-year-old sister, was standing on top of a sand dune, her hand forming an awning over her eyes.

"I see she's back from her missions trip," Fiona said. "Are you ready for her to be the boss of you again?"

Sophie didn't answer, because the sight of her sister made her want to run—not away from her, but to her. *I missed her!* Sophie thought. *I actually missed her!*

She started toward the dune, but Zeke hurled himself at her and took both of them down to the sand, squealing like piglets.

"Sophie! I got a new Spider-Man and it's got a wall he can climb up and I can make him do it and I didn't mean to use up your whole purple marker and Mama said I should say I'm sorry and I am and Lacie brought me a drum from Mexico and Daddy says I can play it on all the days that don't end in *Y*—"

Sophie did a few more rolls in the sand with him before he suddenly bolted up and took off with Rory. Lacie stood over her, her dark-like-Daddy's hair pulled up into a fashionably messy bun. She looked like while she was away she'd stretched upward and inward, and in some places outward. She reached down a hand to pull Sophie up.

"I won't hug you 'cause I'm all yucky now," Sophie said.

"Are you kidding me? I haven't seen you in three weeks!"

Lacie pulled Sophie into a hug and then held her out by the shoulders to look at her. Her deep blue eyes sparkled. "You haven't grown any. I guess you're always going to be a peanut. So, how ARE you?"

Sophie could only stare at her. Where was the *real* Lacie?

Darbie, Maggie, and Fiona were also gazing at Lacie as if she were an extraterrestrial. They had talked Sophie down from a furious-with-Lacie fit more than once.

"I'm good," Sophie said. "Where's Mama and Daddy?"

Lacie pointed toward the beach house, and slapping at the sand on her arms as she ran, Sophie headed that way. She could hear the other three Corn Flakes behind her, squawking as if it were *their* parents who had just arrived. Everybody loved Mama. And everybody understood Daddy, which was basically enough.

Daddy met her on the wooden walkway and picked her up for a hug. He held on to her longer than usual. It made Sophie glance toward the porch, where Mama—who everyone said was a grown-up version of Sophie—was listening to Dr. Bunting. Sophie's stomach tied in a knot. Mama's eyes were puffy, like she'd been crying. Hard.

"Dream Girl!" Mama said. She flung out her arms to Sophie and the other Corn Flakes, although when Maggie stepped up for her turn, she refused the hug and just said, "Something's wrong."

"Sit, ladies," Dr. Bunting said. "Let's talk."

Maggie didn't sit.

Sophie squeezed into the chair with her mother. Fiona hiked herself up onto the low railing. Only Darbie selected her own chair, where she curled up in a ball.

I don't think we want to hear this, Sophie thought.

"Okay, girls, here's the deal," Dr. Bunting said. She ran her fingers through her short-cut hair and pushed up the sleeves of her shirt. "And I want you to hear me out before you start asking questions." She looked right at Fiona. "Or jump to any conclusions."

"About what?" Fiona said.

"Exactly my point. The doctors have done tests, and Kitty has been diagnosed with what's known as ALL—acute lymphoblastic leukemia—"

"Kitty does NOT have leukemia," Fiona said.

Dr. Bunting put up her hand without looking at Fiona. "It's a very serious form of cancer that happens in children sometimes—

BUT—" She waited while Fiona closed her mouth. Darbie sat up straight in her chair, and Maggie doubled her fists like she was going to take Dr. Bunting down.

"BUT—two-thirds of the children diagnosed with leukemia go into remission."

"What does that mean?" Maggie said.

"Remission means they don't show any signs of having leukemia anymore."

"Then that's what's going to happen for Kitty," Fiona said.

"That may very well be true with the kind of treatment Kitty is going to get at Portsmouth. It's one of the finest military hospitals in the country."

"What happens if she doesn't get that remission thing?" Maggie said.

Dr. Bunting folded her arms. "Then they'll keep treating her."

Maggie looked like she was digesting something she hadn't bothered to chew. Mama hugged Sophie close to her. "The best thing we can do for Kitty is pray for her and let her know that we love her."

"She can still play with us, though, right?" Fiona said. "They'll start medicating her, and she'll be able to have the rest of summer vacation, right?"

Sophie looked up at Fiona. There was a look Fiona sometimes got when she sounded like she knew what she was talking about, but she really didn't. She had that look now.

"Eventually she will," Dr. Bunting said. She tilted her head toward Daddy, who was standing off to the side, rubbing the back of his neck. "How much detail do you want me to go into?"

"I know everything I want to know," Darbie said. She was gnawing hard on her lower lip.

"Then I think that's plenty," Mama said. "I promised your aunt Emily we would pay attention to that."

"But there IS more you have to tell us," Fiona said. "Just not now. Which means it isn't bad, because if it was bad, you'd give it all to us right now. I know how you are."

Fiona's mother looked at Mama. "You want her? You can have her."

"Oh, no, not a chance," Daddy said. "She's more trouble than my three put together." He grinned at Fiona. But Sophie didn't see a grin in his eyes. There was no room in there with the sadness.

Mama volunteered to pack Sophie's stuff up for her. Maggie, Darbie, and Fiona trailed after her to get their own things together, Fiona explaining in eleventh-grade vocabulary words what "two-thirds" meant for Kitty.

But Sophie didn't follow. She wandered back down the wooden walkway that led from the house to the beach, draping her towel around her shoulders like a shawl.

Sofia hung her head as she dragged her bare feet along the edge of the Mediterranean Sea, the heat of the sand biting at her soles. What difference did it make? Her friend Danielle was sick. She asked, "Why did God let this happen?" Something tugged at Sofia's shawl. When she looked up, she saw—

Genevieve fell into step beside Sophie. "That's always the question when something bad happens," she said. "You want to talk about it?"

Sophie dragged her toes as she walked, digging into the darker sand that hid beneath the soft golden part. She never talked about God except to Dr. Peter, not about the hard things, anyway. She could count on him not to tell her she was the worst person on the planet for not being sure God knew what he was doing.

She looked sideways at Genevieve. She didn't *look* like she was about to whip out a rule book or anything.

If she did, Sophie thought, *I'd just go right down, right here, just like Kitty did.*

She squeezed her thoughts together so the memory wouldn't get through, but there was her friend in her mind—all pale and limp and hurting because she had a terrible disease.

"Why don't we just walk?" Genevieve said. "Walking is also good."

"What about the brats? I mean—Rory and Izzy." Sophie hunched up her shoulders. "Sorry. Fiona always calls them that so I hear it all the time."

"I think of them as puppies, myself," Genevieve said. "As soon as I get them housebroken and through obedience school, they'll be very nice pets."

"Are you serious?" Sophie said.

Genevieve's green eyes were shiny. "No, but it sounded good, didn't it?"

Sophie had to smile at her. She was kind of like Dr. Peter, only taller, and prettier, of course. Maybe she COULD tell her—

"You can have them back now!"

It was Lacie, dragging herself out of the ocean with Izzy and Zeke clinging to her like koala bears and Rory hanging off her back, all making little-kid beach sounds.

"Slacker," Genevieve said to Lacie with a grin. "It's time for me to take them back up to the house anyway."

"Not yet!" Zeke said.

Rory turned to him, his small face serious. "We don't say no to Genevieve, dude."

Genevieve ushered them up the dune. Lacie pulled a towel out of her bag, which she'd parked on the beach, and wrapped it around her chest.

"You okay, Soph?" she said.

"No," Sophie said. "Kitty has leukemia."

"I know. Dad told me."

"She's really sick."

"Well, yeah, she is." Lacie shook her head like a wet dog. "But you have to have faith. God will take care of her."

Sophie studied her sister while Lacie sat down and knocked water out of her ear. There really was something different about her now, Sophie thought as she joined her on the sand. Before they'd both left on their trips, they were getting along a LITTLE better than they used to, but Lacie had still been saying things like, "You better start acting normal before you go to middle school, Sophie."

But Sophie hadn't wanted to scream once since Lacie had arrived that day. Sure, they had said only about three sentences to each other, but that was still a record.

Sophie watched the sand slide back and forth across her toenails. There was only one way to find out if Lacie had really changed, and besides, if she didn't ask *somebody*, she might scream anyway.

"Why do you think God let this happen to Kitty?" Sophie said.

Lacie set about untangling her bun. "I kind of asked the same question when I was in Mexico. Why is he letting all those little kids be poor and hungry and sick?"

"Was it awful?" Sophie said.

"You don't even want to know. Seriously, Soph—our garbage cans at home have better food in them than what those poor people are eating."

"But why? Doesn't God care about them?"

Lacie loosened her hair with her fingers and dug in her bag until she pulled out a comb. "Of course he cares about them. Somehow it's part of his plan. That's what I learned down there."

Sophie felt her eyes bulging. "God PLANNED for Kitty to get sick?"

"See, that's the thing. We can't go there. We have to pray for God to show us what to do about it. It's like, don't ask 'Why,' ask 'What next?' That's what the people in our village did."

"Even if Kitty's parents won't even let her go to church?"

Lacie pulled a clump of wet hair out of the comb. "You definitely need to make sure Kitty accepts Jesus Christ as her Lord and Savior and gives her heart to him."

It sounded to Sophie like Lacie was reciting the alphabet. She wasn't even sure she knew what Lacie was talking about.

Lacie put the comb down. "We should probably pray for Kitty's soul right now."

"Her soul?" Sophie said. She pulled a narrow panel of her hair under her nose like a mustache. "Why don't we pray for God to make her better?"

"It's more important for her to be saved."

"Yeah—like go into that remission thing."

Lacie sighed and put her hands on Sophie's shoulders. "I've seen it up close and personal now, Soph. It doesn't matter how awful your life is. If you have a personal relationship with Jesus Christ and you believe he is the Son of God, you can handle anything. But if you don't—"

"What?" Sophie said. "Then God doesn't care about you?"

"I didn't say that—"

"I don't believe it!" Sophie scrambled up, scattering sand as she stomped her foot. "I don't believe God won't take care of Kitty!"

"Chill, Soph, okay? Maybe you aren't ready for this conversation—"

"I HATE this conversation!"

Lacie shook her head. "Nope. Definitely not ready."

Sophie wadded up her fists. "I thought you changed—but you didn't. You're still—"

"What?" Lacie said, squinting up at her. "Trying to help you?"

"You're not helping!" Sophie cried. "So just don't try!"

She ran for the dunes, kicking sand out behind her.

But she wasn't quite sure what she was running from.

Everything seemed different to Sophie when she got back to Poquoson. The grass

4

was so un-beach-like, and after living in a beach house that her whole HOUSE would have fit inside one and a half times, her room felt like it had shrunk. Mama still made brownies and called her Dream Girl and tucked everybody in at night. But somehow it seemed to Sophie as if everything had gone on without her while she was away, and she couldn't quite join in again.

It *was* good to be back with Mama and Daddy, when Daddy wasn't saying things like, "Pinch-hit for Lacie on the dishes tonight, would you, Soph? She has volleyball practice." Or youth group. Or babysitting. Or worse, afterward, when he'd say, "Way to take a hit for the team."

It was even pretty good to be with Zeke, except when she found out he had not only emptied her purple marker, but the light blue and the lime green too. Her three favorites.

Lacie was another thing all together. Sophie stayed away from her as much as she could, so Lacie wouldn't try to tell her that Kitty wasn't going to get *any* help from God if she didn't do whatever it was Lacie had said she better do. It wasn't hard to avoid her sister, because she was always off doing all the things that kept her from doing her chores. Sophie was taking a lot of hits for the team.

Mostly, it was hard to get used to not having her Corn Flakes with her every second. One night Sophie even woke up and whispered, "Fiona? Are you hungry?" before she realized she was in her own bed.

It helped to think back and giggle over the outrageous things they'd done at the beach. But whenever Kitty danced across her mind-screen, Sophie stopped giggling and started thinking about leukemia and how heinous it sounded, even though she didn't know exactly what it was. And about Kitty looking so tiny and too-white lying on the sand.

Sofia drew her shawl over the lower half of her face, darting in and out of alleys with the Nazis close behind. She couldn't let them catch her, not before she found Papa and got him to safety. The things they might do to him—

The problem was, Sophie didn't have a clue what the Nazis were going to do to her if they caught her or what the south of France looked like or even if there *were* any alleys there. Fiona always got that kind of information for the Corn Flakes.

Sophie knew what she really needed to do, of course, and late one night after three days of milling around the house and sighing and having Mama make suggestions that didn't sound fun, she decided to do what Dr. Peter had taught her. It was time to imagine Jesus and tell *him* what was going on with her.

It was hot upstairs in their old house, even with the air conditioner humming its heart out, and Sophie kicked off the covers and stared at the paste-on stars that glowed on her ceiling. They all were in the proper constellations. Fiona had seen to that.

"Okay, God," Sophie whispered before she closed her eyes, "I'm scared to talk to you because what if I wait for an answer like I always do, and then tomorrow or the next day or the next day after that you find a way to tell me Lacie was right—that if Kitty doesn't do all that stuff Lacie said then something bad is gonna happen to her that Lacie never did tell me because she said I wasn't ready."

Sophie took a breath and whispered lower, until she almost wasn't speaking at all. "I don't even know if *I'm* doing all that stuff Lacie said—like accepting Jesus as my Lord and Savior—it was like it was all one word and I didn't understand it. I just thought I had to talk to you and try to act like you, because you're the only God and you love me and I love you."

It was getting harder to talk. Sophie closed her eyes and gathered up the picture of her Jesus with the kind eyes and the face that never twisted all up because she was dreamy and silly and weird and a lot of times wrong.

He was there. He was always there. She could always talk to him. Dr. Peter had taught her not to imagine him talking back, the way she had her imaginary film characters do. He said Jesus would do his own talking in his own way, if Sophie would only wait.

It had always happened before—

"Is it wrong that I have questions about what you're doing?" she asked out loud. "I only have two: Why did you let leukemia happen to Kitty? And is it true that you won't take care of her if she doesn't get 'saved'? And Jesus, I'm not exactly sure I know what that means, so would you explain that? I guess that's three questions.

"And I don't care what Lacie says, even though she went on that missions trip, I'm going to ask you: Would you please make Kitty well? Would you make sure she has one of those things that two-thirds of all leukemia kids get? That's five questions. Is that too many? I love you. Thank you. Amen."

Sophie knew there wouldn't be answers right away, especially since she had given Jesus an entire list. She *did* expect the light feeling she usually got when she went to him, like he was now carrying all the stuff she'd been lugging around.

But the feeling wasn't there. She was cold now, and she pulled her pink bedspread up to her chin and shivered.

I wish Fiona was here, she thought. *We'd sneak into the kitchen for cold pizza.*

Sofia could hear her stomach growling. She had been running from the Nazis for so long, she hadn't eaten in days. What COULD she eat? Creeping like a shadow down the steps toward the subway, in case the Nazis were following, Sofia stole up to a trash can. 'The food in the trash cans is better than what the poor people are eating,' her sister had told her. Lifting the lid without making a sound, Sofia peered inside. The smell of garbage assaulted her nose, and she had to force herself not to slam the lid back down. Even as she replaced it, she saw an empty Corn Flakes box. But behind her, something moved in the darkness. There was no time to go back for the box in hopes of a few crumbs. She scurried back up the steps, pulling her shawl tightly around her—

She woke up later with Mama pulling the bedspread off her.

"Aren't you hot?" she said.

"Can we have Corn Flakes tomorrow?" Sophie said.

She heard Mama chuckle in the dark. "You can call them in the morning, Dream Girl," she said.

Having her friends over the next day was, as Darbie put it, "Class!" That was the highest form of "great" in her vocabulary.

Willoughby was still away, and, of course, they didn't have Kitty—but with what Fiona knew about the Nazis and Marseille, the city in the south of France on the Mediterranean Sea, they could still plan their film, which they did over the next three days.

There was a special process to make a Corn Flakes production come together. Sophie always took care of Step One, which was to discover the perfect characters and the most excellent mission from one of her daydreams.

Step Two was Fiona's job, which was to do the necessary research to make it totally real. She had already checked that one off.

Step Three: As they talked about the production—the characters, script, setting, and props—notes were made in the Treasure Book. No one but Maggie did that, and nobody else touched the gel pens.

They were now on Step Four: deciding what the story would be. That was Sophie's favorite part, because they didn't just sit at a table and write it—how boring would that be? They chose their characters and played out the story until it told itself, and Maggie wrote it down as they went, usually with Fiona making sure she got it all in there. At that point Kitty was always starting to nag Maggie about her favorite part, the costumes Maggie and her mom would make for the film. But, of course, Kitty wasn't there. Nobody else brought it up.

For practice, they dried out the ends of the old bread that Mama usually saved for the birds and gnawed on them while they hid between the garage and the line of azalea bushes. Maggie said, as she chewed, that she didn't think it had to be *that* real.

Then they barricaded themselves behind the boxes and trunks in the attic to hide from the Nazis, until even their shorts were soaked with sweat and Mama made them come out and drink about three gallons of water.

By then it was time for Step Five: defining roles and casting the extra parts.

They gathered in Sophie's room, with Maggie sitting at Sophie's desk ready to fill in the names next to the roles, which she had written neatly on a page in the book. Sophie figured it probably took Maggie ten minutes to precisely print each one.

"We need Nazis," Maggie said.

"I don't think I can be one of those," Darbie said from her place on her tummy at the end of the bed. "They're absolute blaggards."

"I'll do it," Maggie said. "But I'll have to change my name. I don't think a Nazi can be called Marguerite."

Fiona plopped onto one of the cushions against the wall in the library corner of Sophie's room. "I'll be one too, even though they were evil and heinous and killed over six million Jews. SIX million! Do you have any idea how many that is?"

"Can the Nazis in our movie get what they deserve?" Darbie said, kicking her feet back and forth. "Can't we reef them?"

"We can do anything we want," Sophie said. "That's why I love making movies." She sat up straight in the middle of her bed and wafted a hand in the air. "Sofia can lead her mother to safety while the brave and bold Daphne takes them down."

Maggie frowned. "That means we have to change the script. It'll mess it all up."

"We'll ad-lib," Fiona said. "You know—make it up when we get to that part."

Maggie gave a grunt and made a note of that. "Next is Sofia's mother. Who's gonna play her?"

"Willoughby can when she comes back," Sophie said.

"What about Kitty?"

They all looked at Fiona.

"Kitty can't." Maggie's words were thudding harder than usual.

Fiona rolled her eyes. "My mother always gives the worst possible scenario when she talks to patients' families, so if something bad happens they can't come back and say she didn't warn them. She told me that herself." She picked up another cushion and hugged it. "It isn't going to be that long until Kitty will be home. Go ahead and make her the mother—Danielle."

"But you don't know—," Maggie started to say. Someone tapped on the door.

Mama poked her curly head inside the room.

"I was just wondering if anybody wanted to go see Kitty with me tomorrow. She can have visitors now."

The Corn Flakes wriggled, squealing, into a group hug, and even Maggie smiled. Mama suggested they put together a basket of things Kitty might enjoy—which meant a major trip to the store and a complete raid of the house. By the time they were finished, Mama's huge basket was bulging with markers, very cool paper, CDs for the portable player Lacie put in there on loan, hair thingies, a stuffed kitten that purred when you squeezed it, and a kit for making jewelry that Sophie had gotten for her birthday. Kitty had gone nuts over it at Sophie's party.

Not only *that*, but they managed to stuff in granola bars, juice boxes in Kitty's favorite flavor, strawberry kiwi, and little bags of Mama's amazing brownies.

"THIS is class!" Darbie said the next morning as Daddy loaded the basket into the old Suburban, because nobody else could lift it alone.

"You better get a wheelchair for this thing when you get there," Daddy said.

Sophie was so excited, she actually clapped her hands.

But the closer they got to Portsmouth, the less anyone talked—except Fiona, who chattered on, the way she did on those rare occasions when she was a nervous wreck.

"I hope they let us all go into her room at the same time," Fiona said, "because Mom said they might limit the number of visitors she can have at once, but we can always ask her sisters to leave if they're all in there. She has like four or five. Let's see, there's Karen, Kayla—"

"Fiona," Mama said as they pulled into the parking lot, "take a breath."

That was when Sophie realized she'd been *holding* hers.

It felt, as Fiona put it, "disconcerting" to be in a hospital. Everything was stainless steel and too clean, *so sick people won't get sicker,* Sophie thought. She was feeling a little nauseated herself. They had to have special passes to get in, since it was a military hospital, and somehow that made it even more disconcerting.

But nothing caught Sophie's breath and held it like the sight of Kitty, sitting up in the middle of a bed that had more cords and knobs than the space modules she'd seen at NASA, where her dad worked.

Kitty let out a little half-scream and reached out her arms for hugs—which were hard to give because there was a tube hanging from one of her arms that led to a bag of liquid stuff on a pole. Sophie didn't want to know how it was attached to Kitty.

They each gave her a careful squeeze and then backed off as soon as they could get free to stare at things they had seen only on TV. Except Fiona, who said, "What's all this for?"

"I don't know." Kitty giggled. "They told me, but I didn't exactly get it."

"I bet I can figure it out," Fiona said.

Sophie was watching Kitty carefully. She didn't look any worse than she had when she left the beach. And she wasn't whining—yet. And she seemed ecstatic to see them, which Fiona said was the happiest you could get.

"All right, Kitty," Darbie said, hands on hips. "Are they decent to you here?"

"I can have anything I want! Well, almost anything. I wanted to order a pizza, but they wouldn't let me do that. Oh, and my nurse on the day shift is really cute." She giggled again. "His name is Sebastian."

Talking about a cute boy. That was a very hopeful sign, Sophie thought.

Maggie, who had up till now been standing with her arms folded, taking a full survey of Kitty, said, "Do you still hurt?"

"Not as bad. They're giving me medicine." She pointed to the bag on the pole.

"What's its name?" Sophie said.

"I don't know!" Kitty said.

"It has to have a name if it's going to live in here." Sophie turned to the Corn Flakes. "Any suggestions?"

"I want it to be a boy," Kitty said.

"Figures," Fiona said.

Darbie smiled her crooked-toothed smile. "I think it should be Hector."

"No!" Kitty wailed.

"Percival!"

"Maurice!"

"NO—give it a cool name!" Kitty was whining. Definitely a good sign, in Sophie's opinion.

"Joe," Maggie said.

They all looked at Kitty.

"Is that cool?" she said.

"No doubt," Darbie said.

"Okay. Joe."

Fiona picked up what looked like a remote. "This works your bed, Kitty."

"It does?"

"Yeah, watch."

Fiona pushed a button, and the foot of the bed began to rise. She pushed another one, and the head came up. Kitty was slowly being folded into a mattress taco.

"I don't think you're supposed to do that," Maggie said.

"I told you I can do almost anything I want here," Kitty said. "Except be with you guys."

Her lower lip trembled, and Sophie could see what was coming.

"We brought you a basket, Kitty!" she said.

"Roll the bed down, Fiona," Darbie said, "so we can give it to her."

Maggie and Darbie hoisted the basket up beside Kitty, but she didn't even get a hand into it because the Corn Flakes pulled out each item and held it up to her and explained it—all at the same time. Kitty giggled through the whole thing and said thank you about a hundred times. When she sniffed at one of the packages of brownies, Fiona said, "You want me to open it?"

"Let's open them all!" Darbie said. "I'm not ashamed to mooch!"

"Not right now," Kitty said. "I'm getting kinda tired."

"I'll fix the pillows—"

"Let me do the bed thing—"

"I can hold this tube deal up for you—"

"You want some covers?"

Kitty sank against the pillows and sighed. Her eyelids drooped over her eyes.

The Corn Flakes stood on each side of the bed, looking at her.

"Should we go?" Sophie whispered.

"We probably should," Darbie whispered back.

"I have to have an operation."

They jumped as if Kitty had leaped off the bed.

"They're going to operate on me," she said.

"What kind of operation?" Maggie said.

Darbie nudged her. "You don't have to talk about it if you don't want to, Kitty."

"They're going to put me to sleep and put a thing in my chest. When I get better from the operation, they'll put medicine in the chest-thing and they won't have to keep sticking things in my arms."

"You'll be asleep," Fiona said, as if she performed surgery herself daily. "It won't even hurt."

Kitty opened her eyes and looked at her, looked at all of the Corn Flakes.

"I'm scared," she said.

All the way home, Sophie held back something hard that was pushing against her chest from the inside, while everyone talked about everything but Kitty. As soon as she got her bedroom door closed and flung herself across the bed, Sophie's chest broke open and let the sobs and the tears come out.

It wasn't long before she felt her mother joining her on the bed and stroking her hair.

"It's hard, isn't it, Dream Girl?" she said.

"You know what, Mama?" Sophie said into the bedspread.

"What?"

"There's nothing in that basket that's going to make Kitty better."

Did Dr. Peter go on his vacation yet?" Sophie said the next morning on the way to church.

Daddy grinned at Mama. "Is that the fifth time or the sixth time she's asked us that since we got up today?"

"Sixth," Lacie said. "And counting."

Mama turned around in her seat and gave Sophie a look that knew things. "I hope he's still around, Soph," she said.

What if he's not? Sophie thought. *I need him to be there! I need him, God, okay?*

It was one of those instant-answer prayers. Dr. Peter was waiting for her at the door to the Sunday school room.

"Sophie-Lophie-Loodle," he said.

It was his special name for her, and it almost made her start crying again. He motioned her over to the little niche by the water fountain. Behind his glasses his usually twinkly eyes were soft, and they drooped at the corners. He ran a hand over his short, gelled curls.

"I heard about Kitty," he said. "I'm so sorry."

"Me too," Sophie said.

"How are you doing with it?"

"Not good at all."

"Let me guess." Dr. Peter wrinkled his nose to scoot up his glasses. "You're feeling anxious and confused and you want to cry every other minute."

"Yes!"

"That's not doing 'bad,'" he said. "That's doing normal. This is a really hard thing to deal with. Of course you're going to feel that way."

Sophie swallowed hard. "But is it normal to be sort of mad too?"

"You think? I'm mad myself. A twelve-year-old suffering like that? It doesn't seem fair."

"I feel madder than that. I want to know why God let this happen." She moved a little closer to him so she could lower her voice. "Do YOU think it's because Kitty doesn't go to church and Bible study?"

One of Dr. Peter's eyebrows twitched. "Did somebody tell you that's the reason?"

"Lacie sorta did."

Dr. Peter glanced at his watch. Sophie had never seen him do that before when they were talking.

"You have to go, huh?" she said. "I didn't mean for us to, like, have a session right now—"

"No, no! I'm glad you asked me. I just want to make sure I talk to somebody before Sunday school starts." He leaned a hand on the wall, above his head, and looked at Sophie with serious eyes. "Kitty doesn't have any control over whether she gets to come to church, so if you think God is punishing her because she doesn't, I don't think that's true." He watched the door to Sophie's Sunday school room close and then glanced down the hall toward the high school room. "I wish I could have you come to my office tomorrow, Loodle, but I'm leaving for vacation right after church. Tell you what—"

He pulled a pen and a pad out of his pocket. The pad was shaped like a lily pad, and the pen, of course, had frog's feet sticking out both sides.

"I'm going to be gone for two weeks," he said as he wrote. "I want you to promise me you'll do two things while I'm away."

"Anything," Sophie said. She could already feel herself getting lighter.

"One—you'll read this Bible story and put yourself in it. You know how."

"Promise."

"And two—you won't stop imagining Jesus every day and listening to the answers. Do what he says, even if it hurts."

"If it HURTS?" Sophie said.

"It just might mean a few sacrifices. Nothing you and God can't handle together." He gave her a smile, and to Sophie it looked a little wobbly. "You can do anything God asks you to do, Sophie. You've proved that—and I think that's why he's asking more from you." He pressed the paper into her hand and whispered, "You can do it."

As she watched him hurry down the hall to the high school room, she sure hoped he was right. It was a heavy thing to even think about doing this without him.

So after church, Sophie dragged a little as she climbed the stairs to her bedroom. A Post-It note was stuck to her pillow.

> *Soph,*
> *Come to my room, K? We need to talk.*
> *Lace*

47

Sophie sniffed. *SHE might need to talk to ME, but I don't need to talk to HER.*

But how many times in the last year had Lacie invited her into the room next door? Besides, Sophie wanted to set her straight about Kitty, now that she'd seen Dr. Peter and *really* knew what she was talking about.

Pulling herself to her full but not very impressive height, Sophie went to Lacie's door, all prepared to knock, but the door was already open.

"Hey, Soph," Lacie said from her cross-legged seat in one of her bowl-like green papasan chairs that swiveled in circles. "Wanna sit?"

It wasn't an order, so Sophie parked herself in the other one, legs sticking straight out above the floor, ready to take off if things got ugly.

"You're still mad at me, aren't you?" Lacie said.

"Yes," Sophie said.

"Well—I don't blame you."

Sophie stared. "Are you serious?"

"Yeah. I messed up at the beach the other day when I was talking to you about Kitty needing to be saved and all—and I wanted to say I'm sorry."

Sophie only nodded at first, since this was *so* un-Lacie-like. She even studied Lacie's freckled face for signs that she might change her mind or add a "But—"

"So—do you forgive me?" Lacie said.

"Sure," was all Sophie managed to say. This was like talking to a stranger she'd known her whole life.

Lacie wiggled to a straighter position in the chair. "What I said wasn't wrong, exactly; it was HOW I said it. Kip said I needed to—"

"Who's Kip?"

"Hello? My high school youth director that took us on the missions trip. He's like Dr. Peter in your Bible study group thing."

Sophie wanted to correct her with the fact that there was *no one* like Dr. Peter, but she held back. So far, Lacie was being pretty decent.

"Anyway, I told Kip what I told you and that you were mad at me about it, and he said that the way I presented it to you probably turned you totally off."

"You mean 'has she accepted-Jesus-Christ-as-her-Savior?'"

Lacie let out a husky laugh. "Is that the way I sounded?"

"Yes."

"No wonder you were mad at me! See, I got so used to saying it over and over on the trip, so—well, whatever—I was TRYING to say that I really want to see Kitty know Jesus like a friend and see that he's the Way."

"To getting well?"

"To living the life he told us about in the Bible and getting to go to heaven—someday. You know, like, when she's an old woman."

Sophie squirmed in the bowl-chair. "But what about now? What about her getting better so they don't have to keep treating her and she can come home and all that?"

"Um, Soph?" Lacie leaned forward so far the chair almost tipped over. "They told me to say I don't know—which is good, because I don't."

"Who's 'they'?"

"Kip. And Dr. Peter."

"Dr. Peter! MY Dr. Peter?"

Lacie looked like she had a gas pain. "Yeah. He came into the high school room and talked to Kip and then Kip AND me, and they said—well, what I already told you."

Sophie felt her eyes narrow. "Did you just apologize because they said you had to?"

"No! I'm totally serious! I'm the one who decided to say I was sorry. They just said to make sure you knew—"

"Got it." Sophie twisted a strand of her hair around a finger as she thought.

"You aren't going to do that mustache thing, are you?" Lacie said.

"No," Sophie said. "I only do that when I'm confused. I'm just thinking—"

"Uh-oh." Lacie grinned and settled back in the chair. If Sophie hadn't known better from past experience, she would have thought Lacie was actually relieved that Sophie didn't storm out of the room.

"I was thinking that if we're not going to figure out why Kitty got sick," Sophie said, "then we have to ask Jesus what to do to help her and listen to what he says and do what he tells us."

Lacie was nodding, the way teachers nodded when it looked like a kid was getting some big math concept. "How do YOU talk to Jesus?" she said.

"I imagine him."

"Go figure."

"But I don't put words in his mouth."

"Right. I have a hard time just sitting there praying, so I write him letters in my journal—WHICH is hidden."

"I'm not gonna go looking for it, if that's what you mean," Sophie said.

Lacie looked startled. "I didn't mean you. I was talking about Zeke. He gets some really bad ideas from Rory."

"Oh," Sophie said. "Yeah."

It was suddenly as if she had run out of things to say. Usually, if she wasn't in an argument with Lacie, they didn't talk this much.

"I don't want to boss you around or anything," Lacie said finally.

"You don't?"

"No. This is just a suggestion. Are y'all still doing a film about the Jews running from the Nazis?"

"Yeah," Sophie said carefully.

"Well, while you're planning this film, maybe really think about the Jews—they had to have total faith or they would have just gone nuts with the fear. So, I'm thinking that could kind of help you with the Kitty thing—I don't know. Just a thought."

"Oh," Sophie said. "Thanks."

She climbed out of the chair and went for the door. Lacie twirled her chair around to face her. "Whatever you want me to do for Kitty, just let me know, okay? I'd hate it if it was one of my best friends."

"Thanks," Sophie said. And she left in what could only be called a state of shock.

Darbie's aunt Emily called that afternoon to invite them over for a cookout. Mama said she could hear Darbie shouting in the background that the rest of the Corn Flakes and their parents were going to be there.

"Let me see," Daddy said to Mama when they got in the car, "do I have everything I need for an afternoon with the Corn Flakes? Earplugs. Tranquilizers. Are the Buntings' two little ones going to be there?"

"No," Mama said. "Just Fiona. We're dropping Z-Boy off to stay with Genevieve."

"Oh, then I didn't have to pack the shin guards after all."

"Da-dee," Sophie said.

"What? What did I say?"

Sophie had everything *she* needed for an afternoon with the Corn Flakes, which was a mind full of the film. She'd called Maggie to make sure she was bringing the Treasure Book and plenty of gel pens.

Darbie, Fiona, and Maggie had a quilt spread out on the grass down by the Poquoson River where Darbie lived with her aunt Emily and uncle Patrick. They were fully equipped with assorted bags of chips, a small cooler full of every juice and soda made and, of course, the Treasure Book. Maggie already had the pen poised for action.

"We totally HAVE to do this film!" Sophie called out as she ran toward them. She slid to a stop on the quilt, narrowly missing Darbie's grape juice box. "You're not gonna believe this, but Lacie gave me the idea."

"No way," Maggie said, as if that were a fact.

"Way. She even invited me to her ROOM." Sophie whipped out the Post-It note from her pocket.

"Let me see that," Fiona said. She took the paper and studied Lacie's handwriting. "She's up to something, guaranteed."

"And maybe she isn't," Darbie said. "Maybe she's just decided to stop running your life."

"Anything's possible, I guess," Fiona said.

"Not that," Maggie said.

Darbie peered over Fiona's shoulder at the note. "So what idea did she give you?"

Sophie got up on her knees. "She said our film could be about the Jewish people having FAITH because that was the only way they got through all the horrible stuff that was happening—just like we have to for Kitty."

Darbie pulled her knees up to her chest and hugged her legs.

"Something's wrong," Maggie said.

"I think that's a class idea—if OUR Jews get to escape."

"Of course they will," Fiona said. "They won't be part of the ones that got killed."

"How'd they kill them?" Maggie said.

"Do we have to go there?" Fiona said. "Some of them got away—Genevieve even said so. Let's concentrate on that." She leaned back on straight arms. "If we're doing this film sort of about faith and all that, God has to take care of them, right?"

"Then why didn't he take care of ALL of them?" Maggie said.

Sophie's stomach went into a square knot. "We can't ask 'Why,' because we don't know," she said. "We have to ask 'What next?'"

"That's what my mum always taught me," Darbie said. "When they threw eggs at me in the street because I was Catholic—"

"They threw EGGS at you?" Fiona said. "That's just heinous."

"What's that other word for *heinous*?" Maggie said.

"Devastating," Fiona said.

"Instead of asking why God let them do that," Darbie went on, "my mum told me we had to figure out how I was going to behave with love."

Darbie sank her chin onto her knees. They all got quiet.

"Does it make you sad to think about your mom?" Sophie said.

Darbie nodded, like maybe she couldn't talk just then.

"Okay—enough with the sadness," Fiona said. She took one last slurp from her soda can and stood up. "Let's get to work."

When they took off for the house, Sophie followed at an I-don't-want-to walk. All of a sudden, she wasn't so excited about this film anymore.

Maybe believing that God was *somehow* there wasn't as easy as it sounded. Darbie was still devastated about her mum. Kitty was still having an operation on top of everything else.

Maybe it was just too hard.

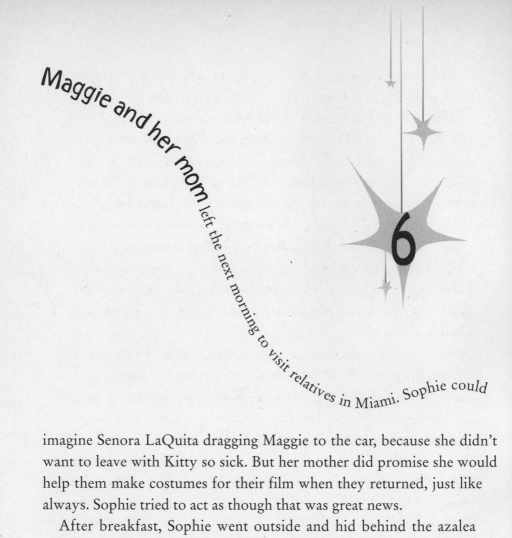

Maggie and her mom left the next morning to visit relatives in Miami. Sophie could imagine Senora LaQuita dragging Maggie to the car, because she didn't want to leave with Kitty so sick. But her mother did promise she would help them make costumes for their film when they returned, just like always. Sophie tried to act as though that was great news.

After breakfast, Sophie went outside and hid behind the azalea bushes by the garage and tried to imagine she was hiding from certain discovery.

Sofia was glad she hadn't brought her mother this far, that she had left her in the safe house where the sympathetic French-man—who had a mustache and wore a blue silk scarf around his neck—said he would keep her mother from harm. "But you must be back before dawn," he had told Sofia.

With danger crawling up her spine like icy fingers, Sofia crept carefully along the wall. She must stay out of the light—she couldn't make a shadow. The Nazis were just across the street, standing guard outside the very building where her father was hiding beneath the floorboards.

I have no choice, she thought. I have to find a way to sneak in there and beg Papa to come with us. We have people who will help us escape to America. She crept along a few more inches, and then a few more, each step slower than the last. But what if they catch me? she thought. What if they drag me off to a concentration camp?

In spite of the perspiration that had formed like little beads across her upper lip, Sofia shivered. She didn't know what could happen in those camps, and she was afraid to find out. Whatever it was, she did know it was heinous. Worse than heinous. Devastating. And to avoid this kind of fate for herself and her family, Sofia would risk her life—

"Soph?"

It was Mama's voice, but it took Sophie a few seconds to realize she was calling from her Loom Room above the garage. Mama's voice came from the upper window.

"Fiona called. She wants you to come over. I told her I'd take you."

Sophie leaned against the wall and wiped the sweat off her upper lip. She had never been relieved to have somebody interrupt a pre-film daydream before, and she called up, "Okay. Thanks."

Fiona's been on the Internet since Sunday, she thought. *I bet she knows ALL about how evil the Nazis were by now.*

Mama pulled the Suburban into the circular driveway at Fiona's, which was one of the biggest homes Sophie had ever been in where somebody actually lived. Dr. Bunting and Fiona waved them over to the deck that sprawled along the whole side of their house.

55

Sophie knew that Fiona's mom never came home for lunch unless somebody needed stitches or had a fever of 102.

Sophie had a sinking feeling in her chest, the kind she used to get as a little girl when she'd agree to go to somebody's birthday party, and then realize on the way there that she really didn't want to go.

"Hey, you two," Dr. Bunting said to Sophie and Mama. "I came home for lunch so I could talk to Fiona, and when she said you were coming over I thought I'd catch you too."

Sophie could feel the sweaty-lip-thing happening again, but tiny beads of sweat also broke out on her forehead this time.

Dr. Bunting shook hands with Mama—most of the time Mama hugged everybody—and said, "Do you want me to send in for some iced tea?"

Mama said no to the tea. She had a little wrinkle between her eyebrows.

"So, I want to talk with you all about Kitty," Dr. Bunting said. "I've been keeping in close touch with her parents, and they want you to know that Kitty got through her operation just fine—no problems."

"Does she have that thing in her chest?" Sophie said.

"Yes—it's called, well, something big and long, but we'll just call it a CVC."

"What's the long name?" Fiona said.

"I'll cover that later," her mom said. She rolled her eyes at Mama. "Soon they'll start her on chemotherapy, which is the treatment for leukemia."

"They'll put the medication in through that CVC," Fiona said.

"Right. The chemotherapy is a mixture of several drugs that will kill off the leukemia cells in her blood and her bone marrow."

"And that will make her have that remission thing?" Sophie said. Her mouth was so dry; she wished Mama had said yes to that iced tea, even though she didn't even *like* the stuff.

"We-e-ell," Dr. Bunting said. "This is only the first round of chemotherapy. She'll get several rounds at different times, and it usually takes a while for a patient to go into remission. All her blood counts have to return to normal so her blood can do all the good things it does for your body, including keeping you from getting infections."

"So it takes, what, three, four weeks?" Fiona said.

"I wish that were the case." Dr. Bunting sat up and folded her hands on the tabletop. "It usually takes at least a year of treatment, usually longer, for remission to occur."

"A YEAR?" Sophie said.

"But that's the worst-case scenario, right?" Fiona said.

"No," her mom said. "That's the best case. For most kids, you're looking at two years."

"Bless her heart," Mama said. The little wrinkle had gone deeper.

"Unfortunately—" Dr. Bunting stopped and looked from Sophie to Fiona as if she were deciding whether to go into this part or not.

Don't tell us, Sophie wanted to say. *Only please do—and don't make it really bad.*

"With most medicine for illness, once you start taking it, you start to feel a little better pretty quickly. You know, like when you take an antibiotic for an ear infection."

"Right," Fiona said. "I hear a 'but' in there, though."

Dr. Bunting nodded. "But with chemotherapy, you feel a whole lot worse when you take it. See, when you kill off the leukemia cells, you kill off a lot of the good ones too, so you run the risk of other infections, and you can get nauseated and vomit, and—you usually lose your hair."

Fiona pulled her head back. "Like, she'll be bald?"

"She could be. Not everybody experiences hair loss, but we always tell patients it's a possibility so they can prepare themselves. That's the least painful of the side effects, but it seems to be the hardest thing for people to deal with, especially girls."

"Does it grow back?" Sophie said. She was almost whispering.

"Oh, yes. She may even have a thicker head of hair when it does."

"In two years?" Sophie said. Kitty would be about to start high school by then. The Corn Flakes would be Lacie's age.

Two years of throwing up and getting infections and going around with no hair? Sophie thought. *God—this is SO not fair! Why would you—*

She had to put out a mental foot and trip that thought because it was way too hard. Dr. Peter said—what did he say about that? She couldn't even remember now. All she could see on her mind-screen was Kitty, hearing this same news in that hospital room in Portsmouth. It was a sure thing that even Sebastian the cute nurse hadn't been able to keep her from sobbing for days.

"Does Darbie know yet?" Sophie said.

"I just got off the phone with her aunt before you got here," Dr. Bunting said. "Emily's mother has had cancer so she understands about chemotherapy. She's going to explain it to her. You two have any questions?"

"Yes," Fiona said. She folded her hands on the table just as her mom was doing. "What are the chances of Kitty going into remission BEFORE most people do?"

"I have no idea, Fiona," Dr. Bunting said. "I can't make a guess, okay? We just have to wait and see."

In Fiona's room, Sophie curled up in the overstuffed striped chair by the window. Fiona squeezed in beside her.

"Okay," she said, "this is totally wretched. Not to mention the fact that my mother talks to me like I don't know anything. Hello! I make straight A's." She got to a position where she could look straight at Sophie. "I think we have to be positive about this. Kitty COULD only need a year of chemotherapy—maybe less, which is what I know my mom is thinking, only she won't say it because that's the way she is. And Kitty might NOT lose her hair. And what's a little throwing up? There are worse things."

Just then, Sophie couldn't think of anything worse than the entire situation.

"I say we just think positive and keep praying and get on with our film," Fiona said. "I found TONS on the Internet." She squirmed out of the chair. "I'm gonna call Darbie. There are only three of us, but we're the brains of the Corn Flakes anyway, right?"

But Aunt Emily said Darbie couldn't come over and when Fiona, of course, asked her why, she said Darbie needed some quiet time.

"Who needs quiet time in the summer?" Fiona said to Sophie. "We'll get enough of that when we have to do homework again."

"Then let's not work on the film by ourselves," Sophie said. "We can't leave EVERYBODY out."

I can't hear anything else that's awful today, Sophie thought. *I think I need some quiet time too.*

Evidently, Darbie needed a lot of it, because over the next several days when Sophie called her, Aunt Emily always said Darbie couldn't talk right then. The third day, Sophie finally found out why.

Mama got off the phone with Aunt Emily and said Darbie had gotten really upset over the things that were happening to Kitty, and it started her thinking about her mom and all the other people she'd lost. Aunt Emily said she could get together with the Flakes again, as long as they didn't talk about Kitty or work on their movie. She said the Holocaust was too disturbing for Darbie right now.

"That's okay with me!" Sophie said. "Fiona isn't going to like it, though."

But Aunt Emily had obviously thought of that, because she said that she and Mama would take the three girls to do some fun things until Darbie felt better.

Her first suggestion wasn't the most "fun" thing Sophie could think of, but at least she and Fiona could be with Darbie. The next day, they went to the mall to shop for school clothes.

Darbie loved to shop, so that made it better. She led them on a lively journey from Old Navy to Limited Too to Gap, collecting bags full of skirts and tops and ponchos and shoes. Aunt Emily said Darbie never got to have nice clothes in Northern Ireland, so she just kept smiling and pulling out her credit card.

Sophie and her mom usually shopped at less-expensive stores, so Sophie acted as Darbie's fashion adviser and brought things to her in the dressing room to try on. Dr. Bunting had given Fiona money, which Fiona said she was saving until they got to the bookstore.

"They don't have school clothes at the bookstore," Sophie said.

"I know," Fiona said.

By lunchtime, Darbie was so loaded down, Aunt Emily had to take her bags to the car while the rest of them got a table at the food court and dug into wonderfully greasy Chinese food.

"I have a feeling the Chinese don't eat this stuff," Mama said as she fished for a piece of chicken with her chopsticks. "But isn't it great?"

"Uh-oh," Darbie said.

Mama jumped and put her hand on Darbie's arm. "What is it, honey? You okay?"

"I WAS—until I saw THEM."

Sophie didn't have to ask what she was talking about. Just two tables over, the Corn Pops—the rich, popular girls from school—were arguing over who was going to sit where.

B.J., Anne-Stuart, and Julia, the Queen Bee. Each one of them had more bags than Darbie, and their voices grew louder and louder.

"Charming," Mama said. "Just ignore them, girls."

Nobody else in the food court was ignoring them. They couldn't.

B.J. could have been heard inside the movie theater at the other end of the mall. She tossed her buttery-blonde bob at the end of every sentence. Julia sat rooting through a shopping bag, seemingly unaware of the other two Corn Pops as she flicked her long auburn hair out of her eyes. Standing with her arms folded across her chest and a pout on her face was skinny Anne-Stuart, glaring at B.J.

"I totally called this seat first!" B.J. said, with a hair-flip.

"Like you ALWAYS do," Anne-Stuart flipped back—although her silky white-blonde hair was up in a bun with the ends sticking out perfectly in all the right places.

Here it comes, Sophie thought.

Julia looked up and seared them both with a green-eyed glare. "You two are acting so immature," she said. "Who CARES where you sit?"

Sophie turned to Fiona and rolled her eyes. She knew that Fiona knew that Julia knew exactly *why* they cared. Whoever sat at Julia's right hand was second in command.

Fiona grunted. "Without Willoughby to pick on, they're fighting for their lives."

"When is Willoughby ever coming back from holiday, anyway?" Darbie said. She called all vacations "holidays," which Sophie liked, only she could never remember to say it herself. "We hardly had a chance to get to know her and she was gone."

"I'm looking forward to getting better acquainted with her," Mama said. "She seems like a sweetheart. I don't know how she ever got mixed up with those three."

"Kitty was a Corn Pop too once," Fiona said.

Sophie glanced at Darbie and kicked Fiona under the table. Still, she had to wonder how Willoughby was going to feel when she got back and found out about Kitty. Willoughby laughed at the smallest thing and made it funny for everybody else, even if they didn't get it.

There's nothing funny about leukemia, Sophie thought.

"Oh, look at this show," Darbie said.

Sophie looked at the Pops and shared disgusted looks with her fellow Flakes. Three high school boys were loping through the food court, and Julia and B.J. and Anne-Stuart were following their every trying-to-be-macho move with their eyes. Sophie expected B.J. to start drooling any minute.

"Give me a break," Fiona said. "They're, like, four years older than us. As if the Pops had a chance."

"Chance to what?" Mama said. She looked horrified.

"I don't know," Fiona said. "THEY don't even know."

The boys draped themselves over the McDonald's counter, obviously completely unaware that the Corn Pops even existed. Immediately, Julia, Anne-Stuart, and B.J. whirled back to their tables and dug through the purses that exactly matched their outfits. Julia produced a compact and fluffed some blush onto her cheeks. Anne-Stuart slathered on lip gloss, and B.J. went after her eyelashes with a mascara brush.

"Cosmetics?" Darbie said.

"That's makeup, all right," Fiona said. "Like it's really going to get those three boys to look at them."

"Hello?"

They both looked at Sophie.

"Just because they talk about us behind their backs," Sophie said, "that doesn't mean we should talk about them."

"You're always so good, Sophie," Darbie said. "Now of course I feel like a complete bogey."

"I just want to say this," Fiona said. "I don't think we're going to have to worry about them anymore. After all the trouble

they got into at the end of last year? They're gonna keep WAY far away from us."

Sophie did give the Pops once last look, though. Even without the makeup, they looked so much older than they had two months ago. Sophie didn't know exactly what it was, but it wasn't the kind of older she wanted to be.

7

to see the Botanical Gardens, to Charlottesville for a tour of Jefferson's Monticello, and back to Virginia Beach. That took Sophie's mind off Kitty during the day, but it was still hard when she was in bed at night, watching the shadows on her ceiling. She couldn't help wondering what it was like for Kitty in that hospital room, chasing shadows of her own. Even for Sophie it was impossible to imagine.

So when Fiona begged for Sophie and Darbie to spend the night at her house one Thursday, Sophie practically held her breath for the whole hour it took for Aunt Emily to finally make the decision to let Darbie go. She just made Sophie and Fiona promise they wouldn't talk about Kitty's sickness or rehearse for their film.

"What ARE we gonna talk about, then?" Fiona said to Sophie before Darbie arrived.

They were sitting in the breakfast nook eating some kind of dip Genevieve had whipped up and served with little triangles of toasted pita bread. Genevieve called it hummus. Sophie didn't ask her what was in it. It tasted really good, and she didn't want to ruin it by finding out it was made from something gross.

"I mean, that's what the Corn Flakes DO," Fiona went on. "We make films and we help each other with problems."

Dr. Bunting hurried into the kitchen, and Genevieve slid a zip-up lunch bag toward her on the counter.

"Tell them about camp," Dr. Bunting said.

"Mom, I'm not going to tell them about camp because I'm not going," Fiona said. She finalized that by stuffing an entire pita triangle into her mouth.

Fiona's mother barely glanced at her as she adjusted her collar. "You go every year, Fiona."

"Not this year," Fiona said with her mouth full.

"You should have told your father that before he wrote the check."

Fiona dunked another piece of pita into the hummus like she was trying to smother it.

"Nobody asked me," she said.

Dr. Bunting finally looked at her. "I thought you loved that place. All the horses and tennis courts and sailboats—it's better than Disney World."

"I just can't be gone for three weeks this summer," Fiona said.

Sophie's hand froze halfway to the dip bowl. *Three weeks? Three weeks without Fiona—right NOW?*

"What, Fiona?" Dr. Bunting said. "Do you have some agenda we don't know about?"

"You don't know anything about what I do." Fiona muttered it so low her mom didn't appear to hear it. She flung the lunch bag over her shoulder by the strap and glanced at her watch.

"Your father already paid the tuition, and it's nonrefundable," she said, halfway out the back door. "You'll be fine. Nice to see you, Sophie."

Sophie could only stare at Fiona.

"I'm not going," Fiona said. "She just doesn't know it yet."

She dropped the piece of pita into the hummus and scraped her chair away from the table. She was out of the kitchen in three steps, but not before Sophie saw tears filming her gray eyes.

Fiona never cried.

Several seconds later, Sophie heard Fiona's bedroom door slam way down in the west wing of the house.

"Should I go after her?" Sophie said to Genevieve.

Genevieve slid into the chair Fiona had just vacated and tucked her feet onto its edge.

"I'd give her a few minutes," Genevieve said. "She's had a couple of meltdowns since Kitty got sick. She always seems to want to calm down by herself." She smiled a little. "I don't know if she'd actually leave a mark on anybody, but I wouldn't chance it."

"Fiona has meltdowns?" Sophie said. She could feel her eyes widening. "I'm her best, best friend, and I never saw one."

Genevieve toyed with her thick braid. "I have a feeling it's because you three aren't allowed to talk about Kitty when you're together, so it gets all bottled up inside. Plus you can't work on your movie, so there goes that outlet. I'm not questioning Darbie's aunt. I can just see that it's hard for you and Fiona."

Sophie put her hands behind her head and pulled her hair into three sections.

"You want me to braid it for you?" Genevieve said.

"Are you serious?" Sophie said.

"Sure," she answered. "You have great hair." Genevieve went into the small bathroom around the corner and came out with a comb and a ponytail holder. She pulled up a chair behind Sophie and started in.

"It does kind of feel like we're, like, stuck," Sophie said.

"You don't do meltdowns, do you?" Genevieve said. "I don't either."

"Nuh-uh. I mostly get into a daydream so I don't have to think about it. Only—that's not working so good lately."

"It's tough to dream your way out of something like this."

Sophie could feel the comb making even panels of hair, and Genevieve pulling them tight in a way that felt firm and neat.

"I could always do it before, no matter what was wrong," Sophie said.

"It's scary when it doesn't work, isn't it?"

"You think?" Sophie picked up the ponytail holder from the table and stretched it in and out with her fingers. "I promised Dr. Peter I would imagine Jesus every day, but I'm scared to do that too. I know that's lame, but—"

"It doesn't sound lame at all. He might end up telling you something you don't want to hear."

"That's totally it!" Sophie said. "Because then I'd have to do whatever he showed me to do, and if it's something like—well, I don't know—like, if it's hard, I don't know if I can do it. Dr. Peter said it might actually hurt."

Genevieve was quiet for a moment. Sophie could feel her getting farther down the braid.

Now she probably thinks I'm a loser, Sophie thought. *There probably isn't anything she thinks is too hard. She tamed Izzy and Rory, didn't she? They're in bed this very minute.*

"Remember my telling you about my grandmother?" Genevieve said.

"Hello? We made our whole film script about her!"

"You might want to put this in, then." Genevieve held her hand out for the ponytail holder and snapped it into place. Sophie got up on her knees in her chair to face her.

Genevieve looked over Sophie's head as if she were seeing her old grandmother right there in the air. "Every time I had a problem I didn't think I could face, she'd say"—Genevieve shifted into a French accent—"'Gennie, as long as you do what God tells you to do in love, it won't be impossible. It might be difficult, but it won't be impossible.'"

Genevieve pulled her eyes back to Sophie with the memory still shining in them. "She said it in French, of course. It loses something in the translation—it was so beautiful. Anyway—she was right. It's gotten me through some really tough times."

Sophie stroked her new braid. "I didn't think anything was hard for you."

Genevieve grinned. "That's FUNNY. Everybody gets something that's too hard for them. Otherwise, why would we need God?"

"Oh," Sophie said.

The doorbell rang, and Sophie heard Fiona's bare feet slapping on the ceramic tile.

"That's probably Darbie," Sophie said.

"Let the games begin," Genevieve said. "I'll bring you guys some smoothies."

Sophie went for the door, and then she stopped. "I like talking to you," she said.

Genevieve nodded the way one grown-up nodded to another.

"I totally feel the same way," she said.

Sophie, Darbie, and Fiona managed to find things to do—like painting designs on each other's toenails and drinking smoothies with Genevieve and braiding each other's hair. Darbie's was too short for a French braid, so they put hers in tiny ones all over her head. The effect was good for fifteen minutes of giggling. There was no evidence of Fiona's meltdown.

But when Sophie woke up in the middle of the night, Fiona wasn't laughing. She was sobbing into her pillow.

Sophie sat straight up in bed, heartbeat throbbing in her neck. "What's wrong?" she said. "Fiona?"

"I don't want to go, Soph," she said in a broken voice. "I don't want to go to camp."

Sophie scooted closer so she wouldn't wake up Darbie, who was conked out on the other side of her in Fiona's king-size bed.

"Is camp heinous?" Sophie said.

"No. I just can't leave you—and Darbie—and Kitty. You guys need me. I'm the one who makes you see that Kitty's gonna be okay. Without me, you'll believe every worst-case scenario my mother tells you."

Sophie squeezed Fiona's hand. "I promise I won't." She glanced over her shoulder at the sleeping Darbie. "And you don't have to worry about her. Aunt Emily probably won't even let her near your mom."

"Pinky promise?" Fiona said.

She crooked her little finger, and Sophie hooked hers with it.

"I take the solemn oath of the Corn Flakes," she said.

Fiona sighed, and in another minute she was asleep. Sophie closed her eyes. All she could see was Kitty, who had nobody to link pinkies with.

Fiona left for camp the following Monday. Sophie guessed that all the meltdowns in the world weren't going to change the Buntings' minds. With Fiona gone—and Maggie, and Kitty, and Willoughby gone too—Darbie and Sophie clung together. They sat glumly at each other's houses, staring at movies they'd already seen and lying on blankets in their backyards, flipping aimlessly through books and turning down every offer Aunt Emily made for yet another day-trip. Sophie was pretty sure she would have offered to fly them to Hawaii if the idea appealed to them.

It didn't.

By the Wednesday after Fiona left, Aunt Emily insisted that Darbie go to Richmond with her for the day.

"She thinks Darbie needs a change of scene," Mama told Sophie the night before.

"I think she needs to talk about Kitty," Sophie said. "Like we do here. It's scarier when you don't talk about it. Everything gets all weird in your mind."

Daddy muted the baseball game on the TV.

Uh-oh, Sophie thought. *This is serious.*

"That makes good sense, Soph," he said. "When did you get to be so smart?"

Even *that* coming from her father didn't do much to cheer Sophie up. She didn't feel smart. She just felt lonely—lonelier than she had in a whole year.

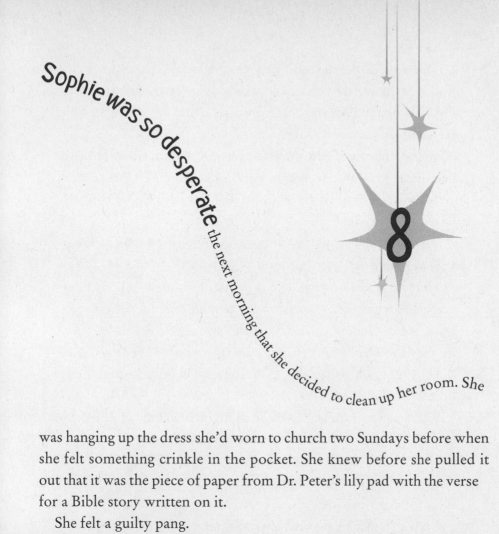

Sophie was so desperate the next morning that she decided to clean up her room. She

was hanging up the dress she'd worn to church two Sundays before when she felt something crinkle in the pocket. She knew before she pulled it out that it was the piece of paper from Dr. Peter's lily pad with the verse for a Bible story written on it.

She felt a guilty pang.

I promised him, she thought. *Dr. Peter will be coming back, and I haven't done anything I told him I'd do.*

So she pulled out her Bible and settled herself on the floor, where the sun made a square on the rug, and leaned against her bed facing the window. "Luke 5:1–11," the paper read. She thumbed through the thin, tissue-like pages.

There was Dr. Peter's handwriting in front of her, almost like he himself was waiting. No way was she going to disappoint him. He had taught the Girls Group to read the Scripture as if they were actually in each story.

Sophie skimmed through the verses and decided that she needed to imagine herself as Simon Peter, even though she was a girl. She knew it wouldn't work if she didn't jump right in the middle of things.

Puffing her chest out to get the feel of big fisherman's muscles, she read out loud.

"'One day as Jesus was standing by the Lake of'—some huge word—'with the people crowding around him and listening to the word of God, he saw at the water's edge two boats, left there by the fishermen, who were washing their nets. He got into one of the boats, the one belonging to Simon, and asked him to put out a little from the shore.'"

This is where I come in, Sophie thought. She drew in a breath and could almost smell the fish-scents, just like at Virginia Beach when they went to get crabs at the fish market. She tried to see herself as Simon, pulling his wet fishing nets from the water to help Jesus. In her mind, Sophie/Simon let the boat drift away from shore.

"Then [Jesus] sat down and taught the people from the boat."

Sophie squeezed her eyes shut tighter. Sophie/Simon's heart would be beating really fast, and his hands would get sweaty—right there next to the real-live Jesus.

"When he had finished speaking, he said to Simon, 'Put out into deep water, and let down the nets for a catch.'"

Simon/Sophie wanted to roll his eyes, but he couldn't—not in front of this man. He had a feeling you just didn't do that. Sophie read Simon's answer to Jesus out loud: "'Master, we've worked hard all night and haven't caught anything.'"

And then his heart almost stopped and something took over his words as if it were somebody else talking. "But because you say so, I will let down the nets."

Sophie was almost sweating herself as she imagined Simon nodding to the other fishermen. They probably grumbled that they'd been fishing all day without catching anything—that it would take a miracle. Or a new career. Sophie answered them herself, "Get over yourselves. He said do it—so do it."

She continued to read the Bible. "'When they had done so, they caught such a large number of fish that their nets began to break. So they signaled their partners in the other boat to come and help them, and they came and filled both boats so full that they began to sink.'"

Simon/Sophie was shouting orders until his throat went hoarse, telling the other fishermen to grab on and get the catch to shore. He had never seen so many fish, all silvery and slithery and flipping over and under one another. He hadn't known there were that many in the whole lake—maybe even in the whole ocean.

"When Simon Peter saw this," Sophie read, "he fell at Jesus' knees and said, 'Go away from me, Lord; I am a sinful man!'"

Don't send him away! Sophie wanted to shout—until she remembered she was supposed to *be* him. She held her breath as she read on.

"Then Jesus said to Simon, 'Don't be afraid; from now on you will catch men.' So they pulled their boats up on shore, left everything and followed him."

Sophie closed the Bible on her lap, but she kept her eyes closed. The sun turned the darkness behind her eyelids red.

I would've gone too, she thought. *I imagine Jesus' eyes all the time, and I'd go anywhere if I could see him in PERSON. Simon was right there WITH him, for real—of course he went.*

Who wanted a fishing business anyway? She was supposed to do whatever Jesus told her to do. Would it really be *that* hard?

Obviously he'd give her everything she needed to do it. Simon had enough fish there to sell and keep his family going for a couple of years.

"Okay!" Sophie said. "I'm getting it."

"Hey, Soph," Lacie called from her room. "Are you hogging the phone again?"

"No!" Sophie said.

"Then who are you talking to?"

"Dr. Peter," Sophie said.

"Oh—naturally—silly me."

Sophie waited for Lacie to yell to Mama that Sophie was finally losing it, but she didn't.

I totally get it, Sophie told Dr. Peter, in her mind this time. *I'm not gonna wait and do a bunch of other stuff if Jesus says to follow him right now.*

Something told Sophie to imagine Simon again, standing there with all the fish he'd ever imagined he could catch, and then some. She imagined how he felt when Jesus said, "Okay, now leave it all here and come with me."

And Simon did.

Yikes! Sophie thought. *I wonder how HIS kids felt when they found out he'd just LEFT. What were THEY supposed to do with all those fish?*

She put the Bible away and plopped down in the middle of the bed where all the clothes she'd planned to put away were piled. She stuck her swimsuit bottoms on her head, just because.

What *would* Dr. Peter say if she could talk to him?

Sophie grunted. That was easy. He'd tell her to ask Jesus to show her what it meant, and then wait.

I'm sick of waiting, she grumbled to herself.

But she did it anyway. And she prayed.

Whatever I'm supposed to do for Kitty, I'll do it, she told his kind eyes, *even if I have to leave—well, not fish, because I don't even have any—but I'll leave everything you want me to if it'll help Kitty.*

She kind of hoped he'd ask her to leave middle school before it even started or run away from the Corn Pops or something like that, but that wasn't much of a sacrifice. Okay, so it wasn't a sacrifice at all.

Besides, how was that going to help Kitty? Sophie decided it was a good thing she didn't have to figure out what *would* help her on her own, because nobody was telling her what Kitty needed. Nobody was saying *anything* about Kitty.

The day was promising to drag itself right into a pit when Mama poked her head in the door to hand her the phone. She looked straight at the swimsuit bottoms on Sophie's head, but she didn't say anything.

When Sophie heard Willoughby's voice on the other end of the phone line, she squealed.

Willoughby was there in ten minutes. Sophie remembered to pull off her headdress before she got there. Then it took twenty more minutes to fill her in on everything that had happened while she was away. The more Sophie told her, the bigger Willoughby's hazel eyes grew, but everything else on her seemed to be shrinking. By the time Sophie was finished, even Willoughby's short, nut-brown curls were drooping.

"I can't BELIEVE this is happening to Kitty. I bet she's crying every minute." Willoughby nodded wisely. "She's always been a crier—and a whiner—but I love her anyway."

"We ALL do," Sophie said. "It's driving me nuts not being able to do anything to help her. I just sit here."

Willoughby got up from Sophie's bed and crossed to the dresser where she picked up Sophie's brush. She perched on the pile of pillows behind Sophie and went to work, pulling the brush through Sophie's hair.

"Everybody wants to do my hair all of a sudden," Sophie said.

"That's because your hair is super thick," Willoughby said. "I KNOW it's gotten thicker while I was gone."

"Nuh-uh!"

"Yuh-huh! If there's anything I know, it's hair. My aunt's a stylist. She owns her own shop."

"Are you serious?"

"She goes to hair shows all the time and comes back with all these killer styles she can do. Too bad I have such lame hair."

"I like your hair!" Sophie said.

"Julia and them never thought so. They were always calling me 'Poodle' and some other names I won't even tell you."

Sophie tried to turn to look at Willoughby, but she had a firm grip on Sophie's hair so she couldn't move her head.

"And they were supposed to be your friends?" Sophie said.

"They just kept me around so they could pick on me," Willoughby said. "Only I never saw that until you guys came along. Being a Corn Flake has, like, saved my life." She giggled. "I love that name—the Corn Flakes. I'm gonna put your hair in all small braids and then put them up in a bun. It'll be cool."

Sophie settled in for what sounded like it was going to take all afternoon. She couldn't help thinking about what the Bible was telling her to do. Arranging her next words carefully, she said, "Do you go to church?"

"We used to when I was little, before my parents got divorced," Willoughby said. "Then my dad stopped taking us because he said he could barely get us all out the door for school five days a week, much less on Sundays too."

"You live with your dad all the time?" Sophie said.

"Yeah, my mom left town," Willoughby said—as if she were merely pointing out that someone had left the room. "You have any bobby pins?"

"I have clips in that box on my dresser," Sophie said.

"Hold this." Willoughby handed her the end of a long, thin braid and stretched for the dresser.

"Do you still believe in God?" Sophie said when she was back to the job.

"Are you kidding me? I pray every night. Tonight I'm gonna pray for Kitty, like, big-time." And then Willoughby giggled, for no apparent reason, which was one of the things she did a lot. Sophie always thought it was the way a poodle might laugh—but she didn't say it. She didn't want Willoughby to think she was like the Corn Pops.

"I'm praying for her too," Sophie said. "I just want to know what she needs so I can do it for her."

"Why don't you ask her?" Willoughby said. Sophie could tell she had several of the clips pressed between her lips.

"She's having her chemotherapy right now, so she's probably really sick. Mama says Dr. Bunting—you know, Fiona's mom—will let us know when it's okay to call her. Except I promised Fiona I wouldn't really listen to her mom, because she always tells us the worst thing that could happen."

"So we could write Kitty a letter," Willoughby said. "This is going to be so cute."

"The letter?" Sophie said.

"No, your hair." Willoughby giggled again.

"You mean, just write to her and ask her to, like, make a list of everything she needs?"

"Why not? My dad always says—" Willoughby made her voice go low and man-like—"'How are you ever going to find out

77

anything if you don't ask questions?'" She went back to her own bubbling tone. "That's why I always ask so many. Julia hates that. She was always telling me to shut up."

"Stop for a second while I get some paper," Sophie said.

She wrote the letter to Kitty while Willoughby finished her hair creation. When they took the letter downstairs to show Mama, she stopped the mixer and stared at Sophie.

"Oh, my Dream Girl," she said. "You look so grown up."

Her eyes turned down at the corners, and for a moment Sophie was afraid she was going to start crying, right in front of Willoughby. She got even more afraid when Mama read their letter, and her eyes got all swimmy.

When Mama finished it, though, Sophie saw her swallow a couple of times before she looked up at them. No tears.

"So—can I have a stamp so we can send it to her?" Sophie said.

Mama shook her head, and Sophie's heart started a downward plunge.

"Let's not send it," Mama said.

"But Mo-om—"

"Let's take it over to her house. This is the kind of thing her parents will want to deliver right into her hands."

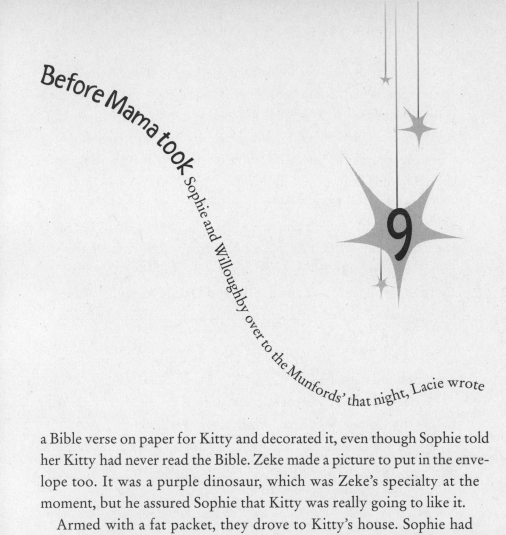

Before Mama took Sophie and Willoughby over to the Munfords' that night, Lacie wrote

a Bible verse on paper for Kitty and decorated it, even though Sophie told her Kitty had never read the Bible. Zeke made a picture to put in the envelope too. It was a purple dinosaur, which was Zeke's specialty at the moment, but he assured Sophie that Kitty was really going to like it.

Armed with a fat packet, they drove to Kitty's house. Sophie had never been there before, and she didn't expect what she saw when they walked in the back door.

"This is a zoo," Willoughby whispered to her.

Four of Kitty's five older sisters were there, and Sophie wouldn't have been surprised if the other one was just lost in the chaos.

There were dishes overflowing the sink and nothing in the drawers or cabinets, which Sophie could tell because they all were hanging open. Clothes were piled up on the dining room table, although it was hard to say whether they all were clean, dirty, or some of both. The tangle of plants in the bay window looked like there was a drought going on.

Three of the girls—Sophie knew their names all started with *K*, but she didn't have a clue who was who—were lounging in the living room watching *Oprah* and passing around an almost-empty bag of sour-cream-and-onion potato chips. When the fourth K, who let Mama and Sophie and Darbie in, said, "We've got company," the rest of them startled up from their seats, and one of them even said, "It's not Dad, is it?"

When they saw that it wasn't, they assumed their previous positions and went back to *Oprah*.

"We're supposed to have the place cleaned up and dinner started before the Colonel gets home," said the girl who let them in.

Sophie had heard Kitty talk about her dad as "the Colonel." She'd also told them he'd had his promotion for six months before she learned that it wasn't spelled K-E-R-N-E-L.

"And you are?" Mama said to the sister who was actually speaking to them.

"I'm Kandy," she said.

"Nice to meet you, Kandy," Mama said. "The girls have written a letter to Kitty, and we thought someone could deliver it when they go to the hospital."

"Sure," Kandy said. "Kelly's going tomorrow—she can take it. Kelly! I'm putting this on the table! Take it to Kitty!"

"Uh-huh," Kelly said. She never took her eyes away from the television.

Sophie watched with horror as Kandy stuck their letter under a pair of jeans that was hanging off the end of the dining room table.

Mama watched her, and Sophie prayed that God would come down and sweep up the envelope and stick it back into Mama's hand—or at least that Mama would think of retrieving it herself.

Instead, Mama stepped farther into the living room and planted herself in front of the TV. Three pairs of glazed eyes came into focus on her.

"Ladies," Mama said in her soft voice, "I have met your father, and I have to say that I personally wouldn't want to be on the receiving end if he walked through that door right now."

"He'd definitely bust a blood vessel," said the K-girl in the reclining chair. "But we don't even know where to start. Mom does everything around here—"

"And now that she's at the hospital with Kitty all the time—" The one on the floor spread out her hands and shrugged.

"It just so happens that I know how to do this kind of thing," Mama said. She gave them her wispy smile. "So what do you say we get to it? I'll give the orders."

They all looked at her as if she couldn't order them out of a wet paper sack, but Sophie knew better. Within five minutes Mama had Kandy and Karen folding laundry, Kelly doing dishes, and Kayla helping her mix up a meat loaf. Mama even unearthed thirteen-year-old Kendra from a back bedroom and got her to start vacuuming. She sent Sophie and Willoughby into the living room to pick up all the clutter and dump it into a laundry basket.

Make that three laundry baskets.

"My dad would ground us for EVER if we let our house get this messy," Willoughby said, "and I've got two brothers."

By the time Colonel Munford got home, dinner was on the table instead of the laundry, which was neatly tucked into drawers, and the living room and kitchen were ready for military inspection—if he didn't look too close. Which he didn't.

Sophie watched Kitty's father glance around. He said, "Good job, girls," and leaned wearily against the wall, rubbing the top of his nearly shaved head.

"He doesn't look so tough to me," Willoughby whispered to Sophie.

All Sophie could do was stare. This couldn't be the same man who had carried Kitty out of the beach house. This guy was smaller and sort of scared-looking, and he didn't bark when he talked.

"I bet I have you to thank for this," he said to Mama.

"They did the work," Mama said.

"I can't tell you how much I appreciate it."

Then he didn't say anything else. It looked like it was just too hard to move his mouth.

"How's our Kitty?" Mama said.

He rubbed his head again. "She's pretty sick. My wife won't even leave her room."

Sophie and Willoughby clenched hands.

"They brought a note for her," Kelly said. "I'm taking it to her tomorrow."

"That's nice," Colonel Munford said. "That's really nice."

Mama nodded, lips pressed together. Then she said, "How about if I come by tomorrow and show the girls how to keep the place going? That will be one thing off your mind."

"You don't have to."

"I know—but I want to." Mama blinked several times. "I love Kitty. It's the least I can do."

The Colonel turned to Mama and engulfed her tiny elfin hands in his. Sophie and Willoughby mumbled their good-byes and backed out the door before the adults could start breaking down and leave nobody knowing what to do. Sophie didn't have much confidence in the K's.

"How come they just sit around and don't clean up?" Sophie said on the way home. "I don't get that."

"I have a theory," Mama said. "Maybe if they just stare at the TV they won't think about their sister. If they do something that doesn't really require them to concentrate, they probably imagine all kinds of things."

"I guess you don't have to concentrate too hard when you're dumping out the trash," Willoughby said with the usual giggle.

"I do know one thing for sure, though," Mama said. "It's obvious they need a lot of help, and I want to do everything I can for them." She glanced over at Sophie in the seat next to her. "Okay—no more trying to distract you. I understand what Aunt Emily has to do for Darbie, but I'm going to let you help as much as you want to. That's the only healthy way you're going to get through this."

Sophie nodded several times. Maybe Jesus wasn't going to ask her to do something that hard after all.

Over the next four days, everybody got focused on "Mission: Kitty," the name of their film.

Lacie got the high school youth group together to mow the Munfords' lawn and wash their cars. They even had a pizza party for the five K's.

"Ken said the girls had a great time last night," Mama told Lacie the next morning.

"Who's Ken?" Sophie said.

"Kitty's father."

Lacie stopped eating her cereal with the spoon in front of her mouth. "Please tell me their mom's name isn't Katie or something."

"Michelle," Mama said.

"That's sad," Sophie said. "I bet she feels left out."

Mama grinned in Lacie's direction "I don't think so. Kendra told me all their middle names start with *M*."

"Don't take me there," Lacie said.

Daddy made up a spreadsheet on his computer so the K's would have a chore schedule. Mama spent two days helping them get rolling with it. She reported that they all fell in love with Zeke, who went with her.

"They'll get over it," Lacie said, and kissed Zeke on the nose.

Mama also made up a bunch of meals the K-girls could pull out of the freezer and warm up for suppers. The best part of that for Sophie and Willoughby was that she got Aunt Emily to come over and help. So they got to be with Darbie again.

After Aunt Emily made Darbie promise she would let her know if she started to get upset, Sophie, Darbie, and Willoughby escaped to Sophie's room to decide what *they* could do for Kitty—since she hadn't sent them her list yet.

"I know what I want to do for her," Willoughby said. "I've wanted to do it ever since I first saw you guys out on the playground."

"And that is—," Darbie said.

"I want to make a movie."

Darbie hooked her hair behind her ears. "We can't do the Nazis," she said. "Aunt Emily would put me in solitary confinement!"

Willoughby shook the curls that sprang out from the edges of the bandana she had tied around her head. Only Willoughby could look good in something like that, Sophie decided.

"No," she said, "let's make a movie about all the things Kitty is missing—you know—us."

"I love it," Darbie said. "Don't you love it, Sophie?"

Sophie was already pulling her camera off the bookshelf.

Before they started, Willoughby did everyone's hair and went through Sophie's closet and drawers to put together outfits that would, as she put it, work for the camera.

"There's still a bit of the Corn Pop in you," Darbie said as Willoughby tied the sleeves of one of Sophie's hooded sweatshirts around her neck, because tall Darbie couldn't actually fit into any of Sophie's tiny tops.

"My dad says there's nothing wrong with looking your best as long as it's not all you think about," Willoughby said. "THAT would be the Corn Pops."

When they all met with Willoughby's approval, they set out to shoot. Corn Flakes piled on the bed. Corn Flakes in a circle on a blanket in the backyard discussing stuff. Corn Flakes making lasagna for the K-crew. But a lot of what they wanted to do was impossible because they didn't have Maggie or Fiona.

I just hope they aren't having too heinous of a time, Sophie thought.

But she knew nobody was having as heinous a go of it as Kitty. No matter how good it felt to finally be doing something for her, Sophie was still flattened by sadness when she crawled into bed that night. She closed her eyes and brought Jesus into view.

I mean it, she prayed to him, *no matter how hard it is, I will do anything you want me to for Kitty. It doesn't feel like what I'm doing is hard enough.*

Usually it took at least a few days for Sophie to see an answer when she really, really asked Jesus a question. But the very next morning, she woke up to what seemed to be the very thing she was asking for.

There was an envelope next to her cereal bowl when Sophie climbed onto the snack bar stool. It had her name on it, but she didn't recognize the handwriting.

"The Colonel dropped it off on his way to the base," Mama said. "It's from Kitty."

Mystified, Sophie tore open the envelope and unfolded the paper.

Sophie, it said, *I'm Sebastian, writing exactly what Kitty tells me to. She makes me wait on her hand and foot.*

Sophie felt herself grinning. She could *clearly* imagine Kitty beaming her dimples at the cute nurse while he took dictation with the pink gel pen.

Sebastian's note from Kitty was a numbered list of only five things:

1. I need more letters from Corn Flakes. I can tape them to my walls.

"We'll write every single day, Sophie said. "Maybe twice a day."

2. I need to see my Corn Flakes. I can't have visitors right now because I might get germs—like you guys actually have any! Hello? I might go mental if I don't get to see you SOON. (Sebastian says I already am.)

Sophie smiled at the paper. The film was going to be *perfect* for that.

3. I need some school clothes. My mom keeps telling me not to worry about stuff like that because I might not be well enough to start school, but if I don't think about clothes then I'll worry too much about what's gonna happen to me next. (Sebastian says to PLEASE bring me some clothes because he's tired of hearing about it.)

Sophie paused on that one. She didn't exactly have the money to go to the mall and buy Kitty a new wardrobe. She and the Corn Flakes would figure something out. So far this was actually pretty easy. But that thought popped like a soda bubble when Sophie read the next item.

4. I want to talk to Dr. Amy again—you know, Fiona's mom. She explains things better than anybody. (Sebastian says what is he, chopped liver?) My mom says I shouldn't bother her because Dr. Amy is way busy—but would you ask her to call me? She's really nice—I know she'll do it if she knows I HAVE to talk to her.

Sophie put the paper down and swung her legs. *I can't tell Fiona's mom to call her,* she thought. *I promised Fiona we wouldn't listen to her mom tell the worst things that could happen.*

She propped her cheeks on her hands with her elbows on the counter and pretended to study the list. But all she could see was Fiona having a meltdown. But a worse image was listening to Dr. Bunting tell Kitty—whatever it was she might say. In that image, *Kitty* was having a meltdown.

Sophie knew she would scratch that item off with a Sharpie if she didn't move on down the list.

5. I need some hair—and not a wig, because they look fake. Mine is already falling out. Sebastian says I look cute, but he's just being nice. I look heinous. (Sebastian asked me how to spell that. Like I KNOW! I wish Fiona were here. I wish all of you were here. I love you. I miss you.)

At the bottom, Kitty had signed her own name. The letters were bravely rounded, and she had put a wobbly heart for the dot. Sophie looked at it until she couldn't see it for the tears.

Why did you put those last two on there, Kitty? Sophie thought. *One's too hard, and the other one's impossible. I can't do this.*

She closed her eyes to stop the tears before they splashed into her Cheerios. And there was Jesus, right where she'd left him—when she'd said no matter how hard it was that she would do whatever he said.

"Is that Kitty's list?" Mama said. She poured apple juice into Sophie's glass.

"Yes," Sophie said. "And I have to find a way to give her everything on it."

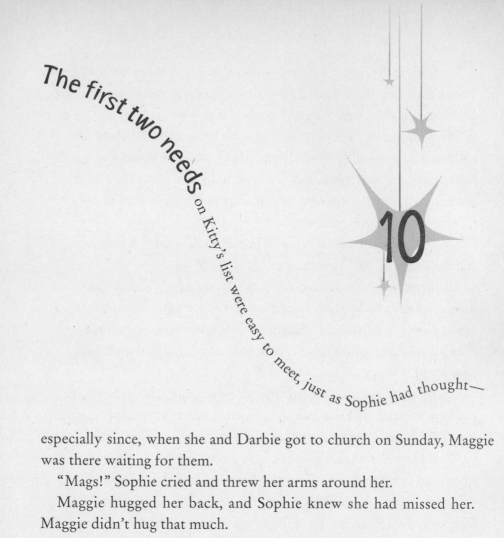

The first two needs on Kitty's list were easy to meet, just as Sophie had thought—

10

especially since, when she and Darbie got to church on Sunday, Maggie was there waiting for them.

"Mags!" Sophie cried and threw her arms around her.

Maggie hugged her back, and Sophie knew she had missed her. Maggie didn't hug that much.

"Get your brain ready, Maggie," Darbie said, "because we have loads to tell you."

That very afternoon they met at Sophie's—Willoughby too—and wrote letters to Kitty so whichever K-sister was going to Portsmouth the next day could take them. They each wrote another one to be opened the next day after that. By the time they were finished, they'd practically used up Sophie's entire supply of stickers and every color of her gel pens.

Then, of course, they added to the *Mission: Kitty* film—*after* Willoughby did her makeover magic on Maggie. That gave Sophie what Fiona would call a "scathingly brilliant idea."

"I know how we can get Kitty some school clothes!" she said.

"Fiona's not here, Sophie," Darbie said. "And I don't think her dad's going to give us his credit card."

"No!" Sophie said. "Willoughby could do some outfits for Kitty using some of OUR clothes."

It took a minute for that to settle in. Then everyone talked at once.

"Aunt Emily is about to give away the things I just grew out of."

"I have stuff I NEVER wear."

"My mom will sew them so they'll fit Kitty."

Willoughby was already headed for Sophie's closet. "I'm going in!" she said.

By the next afternoon, after Darbie, Willoughby, and Maggie had brought over whatever their parents would let them part with, and Willoughby had put together outfits that they were sure would make the Corn Pops drool, the first three items on Kitty's list were checked off.

When they were gone, Sophie sat staring at the fourth request. Kitty wanted to talk to "Dr. Amy."

I promised Fiona, she thought. *But I promised Jesus too.*

Fiona. God. It wasn't like there was a real choice to make. But Sophie gave it one last prayer try.

Jesus, could you just pop Fiona right down here in front of me, so I can at least explain to her?

She even waited five minutes. Fiona did not fall from the sky. Sophie dialed the phone.

"Bunting residence, Genevieve speaking," said the smooth voice on the other end.

"Hi, this is Sophie."

"Sophie! How nice to hear your voice!"

Sophie sagged on the step where she sat with the phone. "How nice to hear yours too."

"I was going to call YOU tonight. I have a message for you from Fiona."

"Is she okay?" Sophie said.

"If 'okay' means she's so miserable she didn't even use any three-syllable words on the phone—sure—she's okay."

"No," Sophie said, "she's wretched."

Genevieve gave an agreeing murmur. "Any messages for her from you?"

"Tell her I miss her so much I'm going off my nut," Sophie said.

"Done. What else you got?"

Sophie squeezed the phone. She could just hang up now.

I could also, like, die of a guilty conscience, she thought.

"I need to talk to Dr. Bunting," she said.

Genevieve laughed softly. "Did you really think she was HERE?"

"Oh," Sophie said. "Duh."

"I could give her a message for you."

Sophie sucked in her breath. This could be the perfect solution. If she had Genevieve tell Dr. Bunting that Kitty wanted to talk to her, Fiona might not be so mad at her.

"Could you just tell her—"

Sophie got a sudden picture of Genevieve taking down her message on the official pad in the kitchen—and Dr. Bunting putting it into a pocket with all the rest of her messages—and getting to it somewhere between operations—

"'Tell her—,'" Genevieve said.

"Could you just ask her to call me REALLY soon?" Sophie said. "It's about Kitty—and it's really, really important."

"I'll write URGENT on it," Genevieve said. "And I'll make sure she gets it as soon as she gets home." Sophie could almost see Genevieve smiling. "If she gets in at 3:00 a.m., do you mind if I give it to her tomorrow?"

"That's fine," Sophie said. "I don't think my parents would like it if she called in the middle of the night."

"Probably not."

"Well—thanks," Sophie said.

"Sophie?" Genevieve said.

"Yeah?"

"I miss you. Maybe I'll bring Izzy and Rory over to play with Zeke if it's okay with your mom. Then you and I can talk."

"That would be great!" Sophie said.

When they hung up, Sophie didn't know whether to feel better because Genevieve might come over and make everything fall into the place where it was supposed to be. Or to go nuts every time the phone rang after that because it might be Dr. Bunting calling.

She was lying across her bed with her head hanging upside down when Lacie came in.

"I don't even want to know," Lacie said.

"Fiona told me one time that if you let all the blood go to your head, you can think better," Sophie said.

"Is it working?" Lacie said.

"I don't know yet."

Lacie climbed up beside her and hung her own head over the side.

"All it's doing is giving me a headache," she said after a minute. She sat up, and Sophie rolled onto her side.

"What are you trying to think about?" Lacie said.

"Hair."

Lacie tugged at a piece of Sophie's. "You definitely have enough of it. Your hair's thicker than mine now."

"Not MY hair," Sophie said. "Kitty's."

"Is she losing hers already?"

Sophie nodded. "And I promised God—you know, Jesus—I'd get her anything she needed. And she says she needs hair—and she says a wig looks fake."

"She's right about that—unless it's a good one—and those are WAY expensive."

Sophie flopped her head down on the mattress. "If I could, I'd give her mine."

Lacie leaped off the bed and pulled open Sophie's desk drawer.

"What are you doing?" Sophie said.

"Looking for a ruler. Hang your head down again."

"Why?"

"Just do it. I'm gonna measure your hair."

Sophie flung her head over again, and Lacie got on her knees and went at it with the ruler. Then she rocked back and sat on her heels.

"I heard about this one thing, Soph," she said. "And I think you CAN give Kitty your hair."

"Are you serious?"

"Come on." Lacie grabbed Sophie's arm. "We have to get on the Net."

Daddy was alone in his study, the glare of the computer screen on his face, when the two of them skidded to a stop in the doorway.

"Uh-oh," he said. "How much is this going to cost me?"

"All we need is ten minutes on the Internet, Daddy," Lacie said.

"Now I KNOW it's going to cost me. Okay, what are we looking up?"

"I think it's called Love Locks or something like that."

Daddy leveled his blue eyes at Lacie. "LOVE Locks? You don't need to be looking at a dating service, Lacie."

"It's about HAIR, Daddy! It's Locks of Love—that's it."

He looked at both of them and then tapped his fingers on the keys. Sophie stared at the screen, her heart pounding. *She could actually give her hair to Kitty? How could that be?*

"Is this it?" Daddy said.

"Yes—that's totally it. Listen, Soph."

Lacie read from the screen about how Locks of Love took donations of hair and made them into beautiful, realistic wigs for people who were suffering from hair loss due to chemotherapy. The wigs, it said, were free to the patients.

"It says hair has to be at least ten inches long."

"How long is mine?" Sophie said.

"Ten inches from your chin to the ends. That would still leave you enough for a really cute bob or something."

Sophie looked at the pictures of the girls with their wigs that looked like their own hair. Their faces were puffy and some of them looked too old in their eyes. But they were all smiling, because they weren't bald.

"How old do you have to be to donate?" Sophie said.

"Scroll down, Daddy," Lacie said.

Daddy leaned the desk chair back and looked at Sophie.

"You really thinking about doing this, Soph?" he said.

"It's for Kitty," she said.

"Hair grows back, you know," he said.

"And mine grows really fast. It'll be long again before seventh grade's over."

"I was talking about Kitty's hair," Daddy said.

Then he turned back to the computer and scrolled down. Sophie thought his eyes looked wet.

"Okay," he said. "Looks like you made the team." He shook his head. "Now all we have to do is convince your mother."

Lacie and Sophie slept on the couch in the family room so they could catch Mama the minute she and Daddy went to the kitchen the next morning. From the way Mama was grinding the coffee beans until they were probably in a fine powder, Sophie could tell Daddy had told her about Locks of Love.

Lacie opened her mouth, a plea already outlined in her eyes as far as Sophie could tell, but Daddy shook his head at them and nodded at the snack bar stools. They climbed onto them, Sophie tucking her legs under her so she'd be high enough to beg Mama straight in the eyes if it came to that. It looked like it was going to.

Mama poured the water into the coffeepot, pushed bread into the toaster, and pulled out a frying pan. Sophie thought she would go *nuts* waiting. Still Daddy shook his head at them and calmly poured himself a glass of orange juice.

Just when Sophie could hardly stand it another minute—and Lacie had her place mat rolled into a tight scroll—Mama came over to the counter with a package of bacon and cut it open while she talked.

"I'm proud of you for thinking of this, Dream Girl," she said. "But cutting all your hair off isn't going to make Kitty better—you know that, don't you?"

"She isn't doing it to make Kitty well, Mama," Lacie said. "She's—"

Mama lifted her eyes to Lacie. "Was I talking to you?"

A chill went through Sophie. Mama never used that tone unless one of them told somebody to shut up or called someone a pig-face or something. Lacie looked at Daddy like she expected him to rescue her. He just put his finger to his lips.

Sophie wanted to pull her hair into a mustache, but she didn't. She had to be clear about this.

"I know it isn't gonna cure her leukemia," Sophie said. "But it WILL make her feel better. I don't even like thinking about her starting middle school with a bald head."

"Senora LaQuita is making her some adorable hats," Mama said.

"WHICH some idiot is going to snatch off her head first chance they get," Lacie said. And then she clapped both hands over her mouth and said between her fingers, "Sorry."

"It's true, Mama," Sophie said. "And Kitty's parents won't have to pay for it if Locks of Love makes a wig out of MY hair. And it'll be real hair and she won't feel like a freak. She just wants to feel like she's normal."

Mama stopped flopping bacon strips into the frying pan and looked up at Sophie again. She looked like she had a heinous headache.

"I think you've done enough for a twelve-year-old," she said. "I'm so proud that you have a heart so big that you want to do everything—but this is an adult decision."

Sophie swallowed hard. She knew what she had to say, but getting it to come out of her mouth was a whole other thing. Across the kitchen, behind Mama, Daddy was nodding at her.

"Actually, Mama," she said, "and I'm not being disrespectful—but it's a God decision. I promised him I would do whatever he asked me to do, no matter how hard it was. So I HAVE to do it."

"But how do you know God is asking you to do this?"

"It was on Kitty's list. She said she wanted hair. I'm doing everything else—I have to do this one thing too."

For the first time, Mama looked around at Daddy. He looked back over his juice glass.

"God didn't write that list," Mama said. "Kitty did."

Sophie felt her heart plunging right down to the pit of her stomach, where it made a hard knot. An almost-angry knot. Lacie patted Sophie's leg under the counter and then raised her hand.

"Can I just say one thing?" Lacie said.

"Go for it," Daddy said, before Mama could answer.

"There isn't anything on that list that goes against what God says in the Bible," Lacie said. "And after all, it's just hair."

"It'll grow back," Daddy said. His lips twitched. "It grows way fast."

Mama looked at Sophie, and the tears came. "Your beautiful hair," she said.

"She'll look really cute with short hair, Mama," Lacie said.

"Willoughby's aunt can cut it," Sophie said.

Mama closed her eyes and nodded.

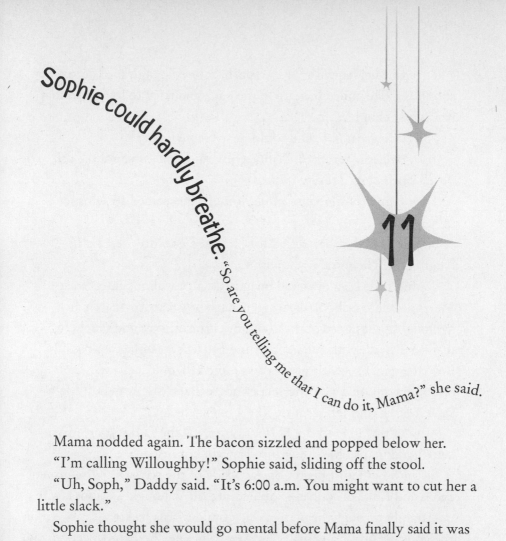

Sophie could hardly breathe. "So are you telling me that I can do it, Mama?" she said.

11

Mama nodded again. The bacon sizzled and popped below her.

"I'm calling Willoughby!" Sophie said, sliding off the stool.

"Uh, Soph," Daddy said. "It's 6:00 a.m. You might want to cut her a little slack."

Sophie thought she would go mental before Mama finally said it was a reasonable hour. Willoughby gave a couple of poodle shrieks and said she could already imagine how her aunt Heather would fix Sophie's hair. She called back ten minutes later and said Sophie was on for one o'clock that afternoon.

That gave Sophie plenty of time to gather Darbie and Maggie. And plenty of time to stand in front of the mirror and imagine herself without the acorn-colored hair draped across her shoulders. She pulled it all up in the back and tried to loop it so that it was just chin length.

You have great hair, she could hear Genevieve say.

Your hair is super thick, Willoughby said in her memory. *I can do all kinds of cool things with it.*

Your hair's thicker than mine now, Lacie seemed to whisper in her ear.

Sophie stared at her reflection, but she couldn't see a chin-length bob. The mirror was a blur.

Sophie closed her eyes and imagined Kitty walking into Great Marsh Middle School wearing a newsboy cap to match her Willoughby-designed outfit—and B.J. cruising past and plucking it off her head, with Julia and Anne-Stuart screaming, "Gross!" until the entire seventh-grade class joined them in a chant.

Sophie shook away the tears and realized she was holding a strand of hair under her nose like a mustache.

"I won't be able to do THIS anymore," she said to her mirror-self. "And that's okay—because I'm not confused."

So with her Corn Flakes on each side of the stylist's chair—except Fiona and Kitty, of course—Sophie watched Willoughby's aunt Heather cut straight through the perfect thick braid Mama had made, place it on the counter, and transform her into someone she barely recognized. When Aunt Heather was through trimming and blow-drying and curling, they all gazed with her into the mirror.

"You're as precious as you can possibly be," Aunt Heather said.

"You look so much OLDER," Mama said.

"I can't wait to try different stuff with it," Willoughby said.

"This is CLASS," Darbie said.

"I liked it better before," Maggie said.

When they all glared at Maggie, she said, "Kitty will look good in it, though."

Aunt Heather placed the cut-off braid in a plastic bag and then in the padded envelope Mama had brought, just like it said on the Locks of Love Web site, just the way the actual person had told Mama on the phone that morning. The person on the phone had also told Mama that the majority of all hair donated came from children who wanted to help other children. Mama had cried again.

But she wasn't crying now. She looked like she was so proud she could have made an announcement on the six o'clock news. She did the next best thing and took them all to Dairy Queen after she put Sophie's hair in the mail.

Sophie spent the rest of the afternoon trying not to look at herself in the mirror every ten seconds. When Daddy got home, he looked at her from all sides and said, "Looking sharp, Soph. Looking real sharp."

"She doesn't look 'sharp,'" Lacie said. "She looks fabulous."

That might have been the best compliment of all.

The phone rang right after supper, and it was Genevieve for Sophie.

"I have the evening off," she said. "I thought I'd come over and see you, if that's okay."

"It's MORE than okay," Sophie said. It was all she could do not to tell Genevieve about her haircut. She wanted to see the look on her face when she saw her.

But it wasn't Genevieve's face Sophie saw when she opened the front door. It was Fiona's. They both screamed at the same time, bringing the entire rest of the LaCroix family running.

"Fiona!" Mama said. "You're home early!"

"They couldn't stand her at camp any longer," Genevieve said behind her. "I had to go get her today."

Sophie flung her arms around Fiona's neck. Fiona put her hands on Sophie's shoulders and held her out at arm's length.

"What did you do to your hair?" she said.

Sophie twirled around. She'd figured out that it felt cool to have her hair swing and bounce around her face. "Do you like it?" she said.

Fiona gave a slow nod. "I think so. I have to get used to it."

"I have SO much to tell you," Sophie said. She turned to Mama. "Can we go up to my room?"

"Like we could stop you," Daddy said on his way back to his study.

Genevieve held up Fiona's backpack. "We brought this just in case."

"You don't even need to ask," Mama said. "I'm going to make some welcome-home—something."

In seconds they were both on Sophie's bed talking over each other.

"I can't believe you're HOME—"

"I was totally DESPONDENT—they had to let me—"

"SO much stuff has happened—"

"Like you making a honking-huge decision without ME."

Sophie stumbled over her own next sentence. "You mean my hair?" she said.

"Well, yeah. Don't we usually discuss major stuff like that?"

"But wait till you hear why I did it," Sophie said.

She told Fiona *some* of the things that were on Kitty's list and *all* about Locks of Love and how she'd had to turn inside out to convince Mama and how Daddy *and* Lacie had stood behind her. When she was done, Fiona still had her arms folded.

"I thought you'd think it was awesome," Sophie said. "It's for Kitty!"

"Kitty's hair is gonna grow back as soon as she goes into remission," Fiona said. "Which is probably going to be any day now."

"I thought it was going to take at least a year."

Fiona finally smiled. "Since when did Kitty ever follow the rules?"

Sophie waited for the Fiona pump-up that always happened when Fiona put things in their right places. But Sophie didn't feel all-of-a-sudden hopeful. She felt a little annoyed.

"I don't think she gets to decide," Sophie said. "Even SHE knows it's going to take a long time."

Fiona tossed her head. "Only because people have been telling her that," she said. "That's one of the reasons I couldn't stand being away at camp. SOMEBODY has to tell Kitty not to listen to all these heinous predictions." She got up and pulled a pen out of the cup on Sophie's desk. "I have to get caught up with you guys on letters—I'm writing her one right now and telling her not to believe all that stuff. She's not as sick as they say she is. I know it."

"Fiona," Sophie said. "I have to tell you something else that was on Kitty's list."

There was a tap on the door. "Phone for you, Soph," Lacie said. She poked her head in and stuck the phone out toward Sophie. "It's Dr. Bunting. I thought she was calling for Fiona, but she said she wanted to talk to YOU. Go figure."

Sophie could hardly take the telephone from Lacie. When she did, her fingers were as stiff as claws around it.

"Why is my mom calling YOU?" Fiona said.

Sophie watched the door close behind Lacie. If she went out in the hall, Fiona would follow her. If she asked Dr. Bunting to call another time, she might not ever catch her again. And besides, Fiona would still ask eight thousand questions. There was nowhere to go and nothing else to do except what she had to do, what she'd promised Kitty—and God—she would do.

"Hello?" Fiona said to Sophie.

But Sophie put the receiver to her ear and said, "Hi."

"Genevieve gave me your message," Dr. Bunting said. "Sorry I haven't gotten back to you sooner. What's up?"

She sounded brisk, like she was already doing three other things, and Sophie was tempted to tell her it wasn't *that* important if she was too busy. But she took a deep breath and, under Fiona's bullet gaze, said, "Actually—I have a message for you from Kitty."

"Oh?" The three other things Dr. Bunting was doing seemed to stop. "What's going on?"

Sophie closed her eyes so she didn't have to look at Fiona. "She asked me to ask you to call her. She said you're really nice to her, and you explain things the way nobody else can."

"Ah. She has some questions, then. Her mother said SHE was going to call me if Kitty needed me."

Sophie squeezed her eyes shut tighter. "She said her mom wouldn't because she thought you'd be too busy."

"Never too busy for this. I'll call her. Let's see—what time is it—it's not that late. I'll call her right now. Thanks, Sophie. Is my daughter over there driving your parents up a wall?"

"She's here," Sophie said slowly. "Do you want to talk to her?"

Dr. Bunting gave a short laugh. "Tell her she's busted for breaking out of camp early. No—don't tell her that. Put her on, would you?"

Keeping her eyes down, Sophie held the phone toward Fiona. "She wants to talk to you now."

"Well, I don't want to talk to HER," Fiona said.

Sophie put the phone back to her ear. "She said—"

"I heard." Dr. Bunting sighed. "All right, tell her we'll talk tomorrow."

She hung up. Sophie took her time doing the same.

"I wanted to tell you, like, right before she called," Sophie said. She still wasn't looking at Fiona.

"Sophie, how COULD you?" Fiona put her hand out and jerked Sophie's chin up. "You PROMISED me."

"But I promised God I would do anything he asked me to do—you know, through Jesus. I didn't know he was going to ask me to do THIS."

Fiona's face was almost purple. She paced the floor at the foot of the bed, waving the gel pen. "So your promise to GOD means more than your promise to ME."

Sophie blinked. "Well, yeah," she said.

The phone rang, but Sophie didn't pick it up. They could hear Mama talking downstairs and then hurrying up the steps. Fiona and Sophie were still staring at each other when Mama burst through the door, talking like she was out of breath.

"That was Dr. Amy again. She just talked to Kitty's mom. Kitty gets to come HOME in two days!"

There was a chorus of squeals, which Lacie and Zeke joined, even though Zeke probably had no idea what was going on.

"We have to get that house in perfect shape," Mama said. "So get some sleep tonight."

The moment the door closed again, Fiona turned to Sophie. "See?" she said. "She wouldn't be coming home if she weren't getting better."

"I guess not," Sophie said. She wished for the first time all day that she had her long hair again so she could pull it under her nose. She was that confused.

"Okay, so I forgive you," Fiona said. She slung an arm around Sophie's neck. "I can see how you'd be pulled in. Stick with me, Soph."

There was so much happy excitement over the next two days; Sophie started to believe that Fiona was right after all. Now that all the Corn Flakes were back together, with Kitty on her way, they went to work at full Corn Flake speed, finishing their *Mission: Kitty* film for her private viewing, making "Welcome back, Kitty!" banners, and fixing up Kitty's room.

They were putting on the final touches when the Colonel and Mrs. Munford pulled into the Munfords' driveway with Kitty in the backseat. Mama had told them to wait until the K-sisters had a chance to do their thing, and then they would have their chance.

That didn't actually take as long as it would have at *her* house, Sophie was sure. Kandy and Kelly and Kendra and Karen and Kayla each gave Kitty a hug and then didn't seem to know what to say.

And actually, for a moment, Sophie didn't either. Seeing Kitty took all the words away.

She looked sort of puffy in her face, and even her china nose looked swollen. But the rest of her was as thin as a stick, and although she was smiling, her eyes somehow seemed thin too.

On her head she wore one of the hats Senora LaQuita had made for her, quilted with a turned-up brim and a silk daisy on it. There was no hair sticking out. Not anywhere.

"Supper's ready for you," Mama said to Mrs. Munford. "Kayla can warm it up when you're set to eat. She has dinner duty tonight."

Mrs. Munford's eyebrows went up. "Dinner duty?" she said. "Kayla?"

"We'll leave you alone to get settled," Mama said.

"Can't they stay for a little while?" Kitty said. Even her whine seemed thinner.

"You have to rest," her mother said. "Or you're going to be right back in the hospital."

Kitty whispered something in her mom's ear, and Mrs. Munford sighed and whispered into Mama's ear. Sophie's stomach got queasy.

"Tell you what," Mama said. "I'll take the rest of the girls home and come back for you, Soph." She smiled and headed for the door. "Let's go, Corn Flakes."

They all gave Kitty and Sophie longing looks as they followed Mama, except for Fiona, who looked downright angry.

"You have to go in your room and lie down, though," Kitty's mom said to her. "And no horsing around."

Kitty sprawled across her bed with a look of pure delight on her face. "I'm home," she said.

"I missed you," Sophie said. "We all did. Fiona TOLD us you would get better fast, and I have to admit, I didn't believe her—"

"Don't believe her," Kitty said. Her puffy face was serious. "I'm only home until my next treatment, and there's going to be a bunch more. That's why I have to ask you something before your mom comes back."

Sophie sat carefully on the edge of the bed. "Ask me anything," she said. "ANYTHING."

Kitty looked straight at her. "Did you know I might die?" she said.

"No!" Sophie said. "You aren't going to die!"

"I might."

Sophie could feel her eyes narrowing. "Did Dr. Amy tell you that?"

Kitty shook her head. "Sebastian told me when I asked him. And the doctors at Portsmouth said it too, and the counselor that comes to talk to me. It's the truth. I could die from leukemia."

Sophie could hardly get her mouth to move. "I didn't know that," she said. And she wished she didn't now.

"So here's my question—and this is really important." Kitty got up on her elbows. "I know you talk to God and Jesus all the time, so you could tell me, Sophie. If I die, am I going to go to heaven?"

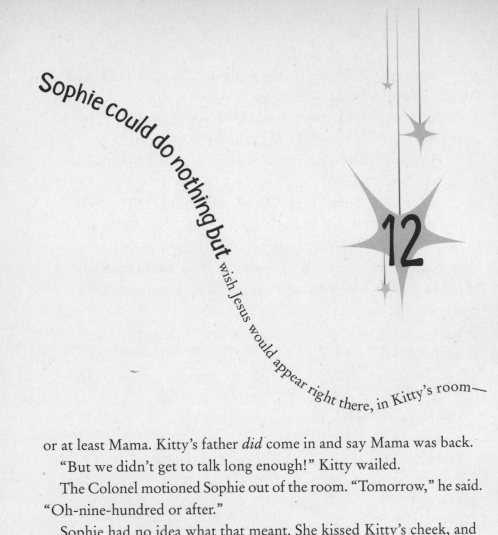

Sophie could do nothing but wish Jesus would appear right there, in Kitty's room—

or at least Mama. Kitty's father *did* come in and say Mama was back.

"But we didn't get to talk long enough!" Kitty wailed.

The Colonel motioned Sophie out of the room. "Tomorrow," he said. "Oh-nine-hundred or after."

Sophie had no idea what that meant. She kissed Kitty's cheek, and Kitty whispered, "Come back soon. I really need to know."

Sophie nodded and escaped.

When they got in the car, Mama said, "Talk to me, Sophie."

Sophie couldn't get the words out fast enough. Mama's hands kept getting whiter on the steering wheel, and she didn't say much until they got in the house and talked to Daddy. His face turned as white as Mama's hands were.

"I just don't think Sophie should be the one to talk to Kitty about death," Mama said, holding on tight to Sophie. "Cutting her hair is one thing—but this?"

Daddy pinched the bridge of his nose between his fingers and closed his eyes. "Okay—here's the game plan," he said. "We call Dr. Peter tomorrow, and we all sit down and discuss this."

"Is he back?" Sophie said.

"Got in a few days ago," Daddy said. "He called to see how you were doing."

Sophie's stomach knot loosened up a little. "Can we do that, Mama?"

"All right," Mama said, although she was giving Daddy a very hard look. "But the final decision is ours."

"Dr. Peter would be the first one to agree," Daddy said.

Sophie didn't say anything. There was no arguing about it this time.

Mama didn't let Sophie go over to Kitty's the next day, and then she said she would rather not have a house full of Corn Flakes because she needed some quiet time to think.

Sophie couldn't find anything to do to pass the weeklong day. She could only see Kitty in her mind, hear her saying, *I might die.*

How could she die? Sophie thought. *She's only twelve years old!*

And if she did, what would that be like? She'd always thought heaven would be a place where you could do whatever you wanted and not have anybody think you were weird. But now that somebody she knew, somebody she really loved, might actually leave the earth—it didn't sound so wonderful.

Kitty wants to go to middle school, Sophie thought. *She wants to have a boyfriend—someday—and have sleepovers with us until she graduates from high school. She can't do that if we're not with her.*

Sophie wanted to say it all out loud—say it to Jesus so he would know by her tone that she was *not* happy about this.

But if Mama heard me, she thought, *she'd never let me talk to Kitty—maybe ever again—*

Sophie couldn't even finish that thought. She tiptoed down the stairs and out the kitchen door and crept along the edge of the garage, like Sofia making her way through the alleys of Marseille. Only this was real. It felt like something *was* after her—and there was only one person who could help her.

She could hear Zeke on the swings in the side yard, shouting something about Spider-Man. Sophie got down on her hands and knees and crawled behind the azaleas. She could feel her throat getting thick.

The last time I was here, I was Sofia, she thought.

She closed her eyes—tight—but Sofia wouldn't appear, and Sophie knew why. It wasn't because Aunt Emily said it would upset Darbie or because all the adults thought the Nazis chasing the Jews was too dark for them to think about with all their other sadness.

I'm sorry, Sofia, Sophie breathed to her in her dream-mind. *It's just because you can't help me right now. You can run away from the Nazis, but I can't run away from Kitty's—maybe—dying. And you can save your father, but I don't know how to save Kitty from not going to heaven—*

Sophie opened her eyes and looked up, over the tops of the azalea bushes. "And you're not the one I need to be talking to anyway."

Closing her eyes one more time, she whispered, "Jesus—is it ever okay to change a promise I made to you?"

She gave a little snort.

"Okay, so that was a lame question. I said I'd do everything you asked me to do for Kitty—I just didn't know I had to do THIS."

She asked him why Kitty had to think about stuff like this when she was so young and why she had picked *her* to tell Kitty whether she was going to heaven or not and what was she supposed to say anyway?

When she ran out of questions, there was only one thing left. It was her image of Jesus, looking at her with his kind eyes.

"I guess you're not mad at me for not wanting to do this," she said. "I guess you know it's hard."

Duh, she said to herself. *He knows everything.*

So, then, he knew what she was supposed to say.

"So, will you TELL me?" she whispered.

She didn't expect an answer, not from his lips anyway. "I should have brought my Bible out here," she said.

That was where the answers always were. She couldn't risk going back to the house. She could still hear Zeke, shouting that he was Spider-Man, and that the enemy didn't have a chance against him.

"He thinks Spider-Man is YOU," Sophie whispered to Jesus. "I gotta straighten him out on that."

Suddenly Sophie's head came up, and she banged it on the garden hose reel.

"I have to tell Kitty too!" she said, in a voice *much* louder than a whisper.

She slapped a hand over her mouth and waited for Zeke to appear, but he was too involved in swinging his way to Spider-Man victory.

Kitty had said it herself: she *knew* Sophie was going to heaven because she talked to Jesus all the time—and believed in him—and obeyed what he said.

"So that's what I have to tell her, right?" Sophie said.

She closed her eyes and saw Jesus' kind eyes. "But I still don't understand why she has to deal with this right NOW," she said. And then she started to cry.

A while later she heard Mama calling her name, and then she heard Daddy's car pull into the driveway—too early to be off work—and then another car. She could tell it was Dr. Peter by his voice calling, "Hey, Spider-Man!" to Zeke. But she stayed behind the azaleas.

"Because what if they don't LET me tell this to Kitty?" she whispered. "How's she ever gonna know?"

"She sure won't if you stay in here talking to yourself."

Sophie jumped and banged her head again. Lacie was crouched down, peering between the leaves.

"They're all waiting for you," Lacie said. "Mama's about to have kittens because she can't find you. So come on—you're never going to find out unless you go in there."

When Sophie walked into the family room, Mama looked at Dr. Peter and Daddy and said, "Now do you know why I'm against this? Look at her—she's upset."

They had obviously started without her. Sophie sank heavily onto the couch next to Dr. Peter. There wasn't even a chance to say hi to him.

Daddy was looking at her like his scientist-self. "ARE you upset, Soph?"

"Rusty!" Mama gave Daddy one of her hard looks.

Dr. Peter didn't say anything, so Sophie took a deep breath.

"I'm only upset because I'm afraid you won't let me talk to Kitty. I know what to say now."

"May I?" Dr. Peter said to Mama.

She barely nodded. Sophie's heart was going like a racecar engine.

Dr. Peter said, "How would you tell her whether she would go to heaven?"

"I would tell her that she was right, that I'm going to heaven because I know Jesus and I talk to him and I obey him and I believe he'll take me up there—or wherever it is."

No one talked for a minute. Mama pulled a tissue out of the box.

"Sounds pretty good to me," Daddy said finally.

"Of course it does, and I'm proud of Sophie," Mama said. "But why does SHE have to be the one?"

"Because," Sophie said. "We have to do whatever God asks us to do—in love—no matter how much it hurts."

Dr. Peter put his hand up. "I told her that."

"And so did Genevieve—AND the Bible," Sophie said.

Daddy sat forward in his chair and put his hand on Mama's knee. "We can't argue with that, Lynda," he said.

"All right," Mama said, in a less than happy voice. She blew her nose hard. "But I want us to be there and Dr. Peter—and I guess Kitty's parents—"

Hello? Sophie wanted to shout. She'd pictured it as just her and Kitty. Why did half the city of Poquoson have to be there?

"I'd like to suggest this," Dr. Peter said. "Just a suggestion— but let Sophie talk to Kitty, and I can be there if you would be more comfortable, if it's okay with Kitty's parents, and if it's all right with Sophie."

Sophie nodded.

"And the two of you can talk to Kitty's parents about what Sophie's going to say beforehand."

"What if they won't let me do it?" Sophie said.

"Then we have to respect that," Mama said.

"Respect that they don't want her to know Jesus?" Sophie said.

"Let's take it one step at a time, huh, Soph?" Daddy said.

It was hard for Sophie not to pray for all the steps to happen at the same time.

The Munfords agreed to meet Sophie, her family, and Dr. Peter at Anna's Pizza for the talk—because that was where the Munfords wanted to go so Kitty could get out a little.

Dr. Peter and Kitty and Sophie picked out songs on the jukebox while Sophie's parents talked with Kitty's parents. After a few

minutes, Sophie heard Colonel Munford say, "It's fine with me. That's a whole lot better than what I could come up with."

"At least we got past Step One," Dr. Peter whispered to Sophie. "Now you can let the grown-ups deal with the Munfords, okay?"

Sophie was *more* than happy to do that. The waitress sailed over with a pizza held above her head and set it down on the separate table Dr. Peter had set up for the three of them.

"I don't know if I can eat pizza yet," Kitty said over the extra-cheese pizza she usually wolfed down. "I still get kinda sick."

"I'll eat your piece," Dr. Peter said. He took a bite and nodded at Sophie.

Kitty pulled her hat down tighter on her head. People were stealing stares at her from other tables. Sophie could tell that Kitty could tell. She wished the wig was made already.

"Do you get to answer my question now?" Kitty said.

"Yes," Sophie said. There was no frozen mouth. No hand squeezing a fork or the edge of the table. The words flowed out of her, better than they had with Mama and Daddy and Dr. Peter. Better than she'd imagined saying it, over and over and over. It was almost like Jesus himself was doing the talking.

When she was through, Kitty looked from Dr. Peter to Sophie.

"I already believe in Jesus," she said. "Because Sophie does, and she's the best person I ever knew. So what do I do now?"

"Oh, Kitty," Dr. Peter said. His eyes were sparkling. "Sophie and I have so much to share with you."

But it obviously wasn't going to be right then. The door opened, and the fading outside light ushered in Julia and Anne-Stuart and a tall, reddish-haired woman who looked around Anna's as if she were Anna herself.

"Don't look," Sophie whispered to Kitty.

But Kitty did, and she put her hand on top of her head and pushed down on the hat some more. But when she pulled her hand away, it caught on the brim and flipped it off. Kitty's whole head, with its few lonely patches of thin hair, was exposed to the world.

Sophie and Kitty both fumbled for the hat, but it was too late. Julia and Anne-Stuart came straight to their table like picnic ants.

"O-kay," Anne-Stuart said.

"Nice do," Julia said.

"She's having chemotherapy," Sophie said. She could barely keep her voice from rising to a scream, or from adding, *morons!*

"Oh," Anne-Stuart said. "Sorry." Her sneer faded, but she still stared at Kitty as if she were a freak of nature.

"Yeah, sorry," Julia said. Something unfamiliar flickered through her eyes. "What's wrong with you?"

Kitty looked at the extra-cheese pizza. "I have leukemia."

"It isn't contagious, is it?" Julia took a step backward.

"No," Kitty said. "You can't catch it."

Julia and Anne-Stuart still gaped at her. Sophie had never known them to be without a word to say.

"So," Julia said finally. "Are y'all coming to middle school orientation tomorrow?"

Sophie looked back at her in surprise. Was it tomorrow? She hadn't gotten a stomach knot over middle school since Kitty had gotten sick. She didn't have one now.

"We'll be there," Sophie said.

"See you, then," Anne-Stuart said, sniffling. The two of them hurried back to the tall woman, buzzing at each other like bees.

Dr. Peter, who had been silent the whole time, said, "Corn Pops, I take it."

"See how heinous they are?" Sophie said.

"I thought they looked a little scared."

Oh, Sophie thought. *THAT was what it was in Julia's eyes.*

"I can't go!" Kitty said.

Sophie looked at Kitty. The fear in *her* eyes was bigger than Julia's. "I'll be the only one there wearing a hat!"

"We'll all be there with you," Sophie said. "All the Corn Flakes. Hey—we could ALL wear hats—you have enough of them."

Kitty shook her head. "What if they won't let me keep it on— they have rules about hats. Or what if it comes off? Or what if somebody pulls it off? You know some Fruit Loop is gonna do that!"

Sophie didn't know what to say. She couldn't make it better.

But all the way home, all she could hear in her head was Kitty saying, *I'll be the only one wearing a hat.*

I've been the "only one" a lot of times, Sophie thought. *The only one who was weird. I know what that feels like.*

But no matter how hard she squeezed her eyes shut, Sophie couldn't imagine how it would feel to walk into that huge middle school tomorrow, already stressing about all the new stuff they would have to do, already worried about whether they would be in the same classes. And to have a hairless head on top of all that.

I don't know how it feels, Jesus! she cried out to him in her mind. *How can I help Kitty if I don't know how it feels?*

The answer came, quicker than it ever had before. When she got home, she went into Daddy's medicine cabinet and pulled something out and went to the kitchen, where he and Mama were getting ready to have their nightly decaf.

Mama saw what was in her hands, and she slammed her cup on the counter.

"NO, Sophie! Absolutely NOT! This is where I draw the line."

"What?" Daddy said. "What do you have, Soph?"

Sophie set the clippers on the counter. Daddy immediately shook his head.

"I have to agree with your mother on this one," he said. "You can't shave your hair off. You'll regret it the minute you do it, and there's no way we can put your hair back on."

"Kitty can't put hers back on either," Sophie said.

"You are not Kitty!" Mama said. "You can't suffer everything she has to suffer! You're twelve years old!"

"I don't know," said a voice from the doorway. Lacie dropped her purse on a chair and came to stand beside Sophie. "I was telling them at youth group tonight that it's like Sophie's not just twelve—she's more like sixteen or seventeen in her soul. Maybe older."

She put her hand next to Sophie's, and Sophie grabbed onto it.

"Lacie, don't start," Mama said.

But Daddy put his hand up. Sophie thought he might drop over any second from the scary look Mama was giving him.

"Let's just hear Lacie out," he said.

Lacie squeezed Sophie's hand tighter. "How long have we been worrying about Sophie because we didn't think she'd ever grow out of the dreamer phase? Now she's showing all this maturity, and you want to hold her back?"

"You think it's maturity?" Daddy said.

"No!" Mama said. "I think it's a beautiful thought, but I don't think it's going to seem that beautiful when she looks in the mirror with a bald head. It's bad enough seeing our Kitty that way."

Mama's face crumpled, and she sagged against Daddy's big chest.

"But I'm not sick like her, Mama," Sophie said. "And I can't make her better—but I CAN make her feel like she's not all alone. No matter how much it hurts ME."

"And it's gonna stink," Lacie said. "You're gonna catch so much flak from those snob-girls."

"I know," Sophie said. "It'll be worse than ever."

Lacie looked at Mama and Daddy. "See?" Lacie said. "She knows what she's up against. She's not pretending everything is going to turn out just fine the way Fiona is. That girl is in total denial."

"Maybe if the Corn Pops and the Fruit Loops have ME to bully," Sophie said. "It'll keep them from dumping it all on Kitty."

Daddy started to nod. Mama pounded her fist weakly on his chest, and then she looked up at Sophie.

"Are you sure, Soph—are you really SURE?"

Sophie just picked up the clippers and climbed up onto a stool.

Daddy took them from her, and Mama wrapped a towel around her shoulders.

"At least you have a decent-shaped head," Lacie said. "You might not look that bad. It'll make your eyes look bigger."

Lacie kept on talking while Sophie watched her reflection in the oven door; watched as her shiny scalp appeared.

She imagined Jesus watching too.

With his kind, approving eyes.

Glossary

ad lib {add-lib} when you act in a movie or play without a script, and make lines up on the spot

agenda {a-jen-duh} a series of plans or ideas that can control someone's actions

ALL (acute lymphoblastic leukemia) {a-cute limp-fo-blast-ick loo-KEY-me-uh} a type of cancer that attacks the white blood cells that normally fight infections. ALL creates white blood cells that can't fight off infections and makes the person very sick. ALL is the most common cancer in children.

au pair {oh-PARE} a fancy French word for a nanny; specifically a young person who lives with a family and takes care of the kids and the housework

blackguards {BLAK-gards} very rude and nasty people

bogey {BO-ghee} an Irish slang word that actually means snot (gross!), but basically tells people you feel really stupid

chemotherapy {key-moe-THAIR-a-pee} really strong chemicals that are used as a treatment for cancer

class {klas} not a group of students, but a nifty word that means something's really cool

CVC an abbreviation of cardiovascular ventricular catheter {car-dee-oh-VAS-cu-lar ven-TRI-cue-lar CATH-et-er}, or a fancy tube through which medicine is put into the body

despondent {de-SPOHN-dent} feeling completely depressed, to the point that you become almost zombie-like

desperate {DEHS-pret} without hope, sometimes doing extreme things to avoid a certain situation or thought

devastating {DEV-as-tate-ing} when an event is so awful and unimaginable that it makes you feel helpless

disconcerting {dis-cohn-CERT-ing} a word that describes something that just doesn't seem right, and makes you feel awkward and confused

ecstatic {ek-sta-tik} so incredibly happy it makes you almost crazy with joy

extraterrestrial {ex-trah-ter-RES-tree-all} something from outer space, or something so strange it seems like it came from outside this world

flitters {FLIT-turs} a feeling of being really excited and a little jumpy, and your body gets a little shaky while you wait for something to happen

heinous {HEY-nus} unbelievably mean and cruel

holiday {HA-leh-day} a British word for vacation

inquisitive {in-KWI-zeh-tiv} being really curious, and asking a lot of questions

liberty {li-burr-tee} freedom; "not at liberty" means you're not allowed, like to say or do something

meltdown {MELT-doun} something that happens when things become too much to handle; losing control of yourself because of the stress

oh-nine-hundred {oh-nyne-hun-dread} 9:00 am in military speak

reef {rEEf} an Irish word that means to attack someone with your words

remission {re-MEH-shon} the time when cancer symptoms aren't active and the person starts to get better

scathingly {SKATH-ing-lee} according to Darbie, wonderfully brilliant

two-thirds {too-therds} approximately 66 percent

scenario {see-NAIR-e-oh} a series of events that could occur; worst case scenarios are they worst possible things that could happen

faiThGirLz!
2 corinthians 4:18

No Boys allowed

Devotions for Girls

Make it happen girl

Take a quiz!

Conquer the green-eyed monster

By Kristi Holl
with Jennifer Vogtlin

Zonderkidz

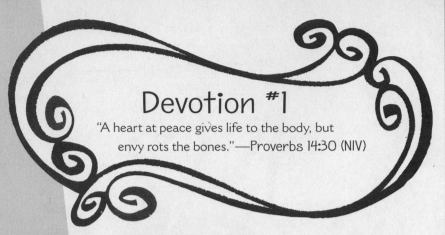

Devotion #1

"A heart at peace gives life to the body, but
envy rots the bones."—Proverbs 14:30 (NIV)

The Green-Eyed Monster

A peaceful heart is relaxed and easy, not tense
and fearful. This peace of mind and heart will
actually give you a longer, healthier life. But envy and
jealousy gnaw at you, deep inside. The Bible says it can
even rot your bones. That's pretty unhealthy!

Envy and jealousy can take you totally by surprise. You
see your dad holding your little step-sister or hugging his new
wife. The stab of jealousy can jab hard. Or maybe it's a milder
form of envy. You'd give anything for your classmate's designer
jeans. Instead, you wear big sister's hand-me-downs and
shop at thrift stores.

These are perfectly innocent moments, but how you
feel during these times—and what you do about it—
is what counts.

Jealousy is sneaky. It's natural to compare
ourselves to others or want what someone else has. But when that comparison
makes us unhappy, we're probably feeling jealous. Notice how you feel about
the good fortune of others: their cool
clothes, perfect looks, or their attention in
the spotlight. If you feel anything but peace

in your heart, you might be feeling jealous. Can you be happy for them instead? Can you compliment them on an outstanding performance or their pretty outfit? Taking positive action is a quick way to kill that green-eyed monster.

The Bible says in James 3:16 that where you have envy (which is another word for jealousy), you will find disorder and every evil practice. Not good! The sooner you tackle these emotions, the easier they are to defeat. God wants you to have a heart filled with peace. A heart at peace is a heart focused on God. So the next time you feel jealous, ask God to help you put jealousy in its place—out of your life!

Did You Know

. . . you can read about jealousy in Genesis 37? When Joseph's half-brothers envied his fancy clothes and were jealous of Joseph's special attention, their evil actions changed history!

More To Explore: Read James 3:13–18

Girl Talk:

Are you jealous of someone? Be honest with yourself, but more importantly, be honest with God. He will help you overcome jealousy.

God Talk:

Lord, I am really jealous of _____. I know that I shouldn't be, but I am. Forgive me. Please help me to love this person like you do. Thank you for all the good things in my life. Help me to focus on all the blessings I already have instead of envying the blessings of others. And thank you for blessing _____. I know you have more than enough blessings to go around. Amen.

Devotion #2

"What is the price of five sparrows? A couple of pennies? Yet God does not forget a single one of them. And the very hairs on your head are all numbered. So don't be afraid; you are more valuable to him than a whole flock of sparrows."—Luke 12:6–7 (NLT)

Million Dollar Hair

If God cares for small birds that are worth only a couple pennies, then imagine how much more he cares for you. He watches over you so closely that he even knows how many hairs you have on your head. You don't ever need to be afraid. God says you are *valuable*: of great worth, precious, and priceless!

Get outside for a minute. Watch the birds overhead as they glide on the breeze without a care in the world. They aren't worried about where their next worm is coming from! "Look at the birds. They don't need to plant or harvest or put food in barns because your heavenly Father feeds them. And you are far more valuable to him than they are." (Matthew 6:26 NLT) If God provides every need for the birds, how much more will he take care of you?

Thinking deeply about this truth can help when you feel sad and lonely, when you think no one notices you. If he is concerned enough to count every hair on your head, then God is even more concerned about your nightmares, that fight with your friend, your dream of being a nurse, and yes, even your frizzy hair. God—the Creator of the whole universe—cares deeply and personally about *you*.

You are precious to God!

Did You Know

. . . that even David, great king of Israel and close friend to God, felt unimportant and overlooked at times? Read Psalm 13.

God Talk:

"Lord, I'm feeling all alone today. I don't know why I'm so valuable to you, but I thank you for your unfailing love. Please help me remember how much you care for me. Amen."

More To Explore: Luke 12:22–31

Girl Talk:

Have you ever felt lonely, even if you're around by family or friends? Take a walk in a park, or look through a nature magazine, to remind you that God takes care of everything in this world, including you! It's a perfect time to ask God to fill you with his love.

Fun Factoid:

An average head has approximately 100,000 hairs on it. Redheads have about 90,000 hairs. Brunettes have about 110,000 hairs, and blondes have about 140,000 hairs.

faiThGirLz!™

Faithgirlz!™—Inner Beauty, Outward Faith

Sophie's World (Book 1)
Written by Nancy Rue
Softcover 0-310-70756-0

Sophie's Secret (Book 2)
Written by Nancy Rue
Softcover 0-310-70757-9

Sophie and the Scoundrels (Book 3)
Written by Nancy Rue
Softcover 0-310-70758-7

Sophie's Irish Showdown (Book 4)
Written by Nancy Rue
Softcover 0-310-70759-5

Sophie's First Dance? (Book 5)
Written by Nancy Rue
Softcover 0-310-70760-9

Sophie's Stormy Summer (Book 6)
Written by Nancy Rue
Softcover 0-310-70761-7

No Boys Allowed: Devotions for Girls
Written by Kristi Holl
Softcover 0-310-70718-8

Available now or coming soon to your local bookstore!

Zonderkidz.

faThGirLz!

Faithgirlz!™—Inner Beauty, Outward Faith

COMING
SOON

Sophie Breaks the Code (Book 7)
Written by Nancy Rue
Softcover 0-310-71022-7

Sophie Tracks a Thief (Book 8)
Written by Nancy Rue
Softcover 0-310-71023-5

Girlz Rock
Written by Nancy Rue
Softcover 0-310-70899-0

Available now or coming soon to your local bookstore!

Zonder**kidz**®

We want to hear from you. Please send your comments about this book to us in care of zreview@zondervan.com. Thank you.

Zonderkidz.

Grand Rapids, MI 49530
www.zonderkidz.com